GW00870050

Twelve Horses
for
JULIA

The story of a southern
Alberta pioneer

Lara Malmqvist

 FriesenPress

Suite 300 - 990 Fort St
Victoria, BC, V8V 3K2
Canada

www.friesenpress.com

Copyright © 2019 by Lara Malmqvist
First Edition — 2019

All rights reserved.

No part of this publication may be reproduced in any form, or by any means, electronic or mechanical, including photocopying, recording, or any information browsing, storage, or retrieval system, without permission in writing from FriesenPress.

Cover art by Marrieta Gal

ISBN
978-1-5255-4531-3 (Hardcover)
978-1-5255-4532-0 (Paperback)
978-1-5255-4533-7 (eBook)

1. Fiction, Historical

Distributed to the trade by The Ingram Book Company

To my mother

CHAPTER 1

Papa's outstretched arm stopped me in my tracks. I drew behind him. At the mouth of the cave, he cocked his pistol and aimed it into the dark cavern that was carved into the bluffs behind our farmhouse. It was cool and dark in the summer's heat and big enough to shelter at least a half-dozen people.

"Git out of there!" Papa growled into the darkness.

I crouched in the prickles, making myself small as Papa shouted.

"I know you're in there, Picard!"

There was a shuffling sound inside the cave, and a man appeared. His hands were held up mockingly near his shoulders and one of his eyes was squinted shut against the blinding sun at the cave's entrance.

"Where'd you hide 'em?" Picard sneered, revealing the decaying stumps of rotting teeth. He eyed Papa and then glanced over to where I knelt.

I pressed myself into the side of the hill and could hear my heart pounding in my ears.

Paul Picard was a notorious thief who had, by chance, stumbled upon runaway slaves hidden in the cold-room cave on one of his thievery sprees at our farm last spring. Aware of the reward for their recapture, Paul galloped away to notify the slave posse that was scouring the groves, thickets, and tall grasses nearby.

Papa witnessed the man's hasty departure and acted swiftly. He loaded the escapees into a wagon with a false bottom and moved them on to a safer location, undetected. And when Paul returned to the farm with members of the posse, the cave was empty. They scoured the farm, but their search was in vain.

Paul was livid. Papa had prevented him from claiming a piece of the reward money, and he sought revenge. He began blackmailing Papa in exchange for his silence. Even in a free state like Iowa, anyone caught aiding escapees was subject to fines and even jail time. But this didn't deter Papa. He regularly attended the anti-slavery and abolitionist meetings held in Taber, and resolved to help people persecuted by their heritage.

"Git off my land!" Papa snarled at Picard. "Before I call the sheriff!"

"The sheriff!" Picard snorted. "He ain't gonna help you! Not after what I tell 'im!"

"Why you–" Papa lunged at him.

But Picard dodged out of the way and ran down the hill. A horse whinnied from a grove of trees a short distance from the base of the hill. Picard ran to it, untied the horse from a tree, and then galloped off the property.

Papa stormed toward the house, muttering to himself. I jogged beside him, trying to keep up through the long grass, which was still damp from the morning showers. The sun had broken through the clouds and beat down on the back of my neck. Mama would scold me later for forgetting my hat again. "You're old enough to remember," she'd tell me. I was eight years old, but every day since the beginning of summer, on my way outside, I'd forgotten to grab my hat off the peg near the door. Although Mama said that I was the spitting image of her, with long dark hair, prominent cheekbones, and dark eyes, my skin was fairer, like Papa's. But under the sun's warm rays, I would tan as dark as a ripe berry, and Mama was always reminding me to cover up.

"Don't grow up to be a bully," Papa said, looking at me sternly, his deep-set blue eyes shadowed by his knitted black brows.

"Okay, Papa," I answered, breathlessly.

"Don't lie," he continued. "And never steal!"

He threw open the screen door, sending it crashing into the kitchen wall.

"Good heavens, Peter." Mama frowned, looking up from the pie dough she was rolling into a circle on the wooden kitchen table, which was dusted with flour. "One of these days, you're going to tear that door right off its hinges. What's got into you?"

I scrambled into the house after him and quietly closed the door, then took a seat on the kitchen chair near Mama.

"He was in the cave again!" Papa bellowed.

"Picard?" Mama asked.

Papa ignored her.

"Trespassing in our cave. Again!" Papa spat and began pacing back and forth.

Mama set aside the rolling pin and looked at me.

"Picard?"

I nodded.

She shook her head, and then began folding the flat piece of dough in half and then in half again. She placed it onto the pie plate, then gently unfolded the dough. Her face was flushed, and a few strands of dark hair escaped from her tidy bun, clinging to the perspiration on her brow. She absently pushed at the strands with the back of her wrist.

"No apples?" she asked me quietly, looking at me with raised eyebrows.

I shook my head. Papa and I had been on our way to the cave to retrieve a basket of apples when we'd met up with Picard.

She rolled her eyes and then began pressing the dough gently against the bottom and sides of the pie plate.

I stared at the trail of footprints Papa's wet boots were making across Mama's freshly scrubbed floor. I looked up at Mama, waiting for her to start yelling like she did when one of my brothers tracked mud or water onto the floors.

Mama didn't even seem to notice. Instead, her face fell and the colour drained from her cheeks as she clutched her belly. She looked as if she was in pain. She was going to have a baby, and it looked like she was going to have it right there and then. I jumped up from my chair and took hold of her arm, guiding her to the seat that I'd vacated.

"It's okay," she said, waving me away. "I just need to sit."

I took over the pie for her, pressing the dough against the plate and using a knife to trim the excess dough that hung over the top.

"This blackmailing has to end!" Papa declared, ignoring Mama's apparent discomfort.

He spun on his heel and stormed out the door, slamming it shut and knocking Mama's painting off the wall, sending it crashing to the floor.

"Oh, that man," Mama huffed, staring at the painting on the floor. She stood up, pulled a basket off the shelf, and then started for the door. "And how can I make an apple pie without apples?"

Papa wasn't deterred by the blackmailing. If anything, it deepened his resolve to help people persecuted because of their race, and he continued to harbour escapees at our farm.

A few weeks after discovering Picard in the cave, I walked into my bedroom and found myself staring into the scared, dark eyes of an older woman with greying hair, and a girl about the same age as Alex, my eldest brother. I stifled a scream with my hand, and then ran to the barn to find Papa.

"There are people hiding in my bedroom!" I cried.

"Hush!" Papa replied angrily, glancing nervously over his shoulder. "Go do your chores."

"But Papa."

"Now!" he barked.

When I returned to my bedroom later that afternoon, after finishing my chores, my room was empty.

Like clockwork, Picard returned to our farm about a month later. I recognized the familiar sound of his wagon rolling down our road and ran to the window.

"He's back, Mama!" I called, over my shoulder.

"Who is?"

"Picard!" I whispered, loudly.

Mama sighed in exasperation, dried her hands on a tea towel, and walked to the window.

Picard stopped his wagon in front of the barn and began loading baskets of freshly picked vegetables onto it. Then Papa appeared from the back of the barn. He quietly crept towards Picard along the drive at the side of the barn, which was still cast in early morning shadows.

"What's he doing?" Mama asked absently, staring at Papa.

At that moment, Papa ran forward, pounced on Picard, and threw him to the ground. Although taken by surprise, Picard quickly recovered, and they began striking at each other furiously as they wrestled and rolled around in the dirt. Then Picard shoved Papa away, jumped to his feet, and pulled out a knife.

"Papa!" I screamed, and moved away from the window, covering my eyes.

Then the sound of a firing gun echoed in my ears.

CHAPTER 2

"Whoa!"

The riders called to their horses, pulling back sharply on the reins and twisting their horses' heads up and back. The horses snorted and danced nervously, as the cloud of dust kicked up by their galloping hooves enveloped them. There were five riders, and each one had a gun at their waist.

"Oh, dear Lord," Mama gasped.

She'd run out onto the porch, with me in tow, after the gunshot rang out. We were then joined by my brothers.

"Who are they?" I asked quietly, grabbing hold of Mama's skirt.

"The sheriff," Mama hushed, "and his slave-hunting posse."

They'd stopped their horses short of Papa, who stood over Picard's lifeless, prone body, holding tightly onto a gun.

"What's that?" I asked, pointing to the crimson red colour that was creeping over the back of Picard's shirt.

"It's blood," she replied, grimacing, and then clutching at her belly.

"Alex," I whispered loudly to my eldest brother.

He turned and glared at me.

"What!" he mouthed

"The baby!" I pointed to Mama's belly.

Alex glanced up at the pained expression on Mama's face, and his look of anger vanished. Grabbing hold of Mama's arm, he guided her to the rocking chair at the side of the porch steps.

"I'm fine," she told him, waving him away.

I followed and stood next to her chair.

"He was stealing again," Papa told the sheriff, who swaggered toward him, his spurs jingling with each step.

The sheriff bent over the body, then straightened up and scratched at the stubble on his craggy cheek.

"You killed 'im," he growled, stretching his hand out towards Papa. "Gimme yer gun."

A yellow butterfly with black stripes fluttered past me, landing on the spiny centre of a coneflower with light purple petals that pointed towards the ground. The butterfly slowly fanned its wings open and closed in the warm morning sunshine, drinking the nectar from the tall flowers that grew below the kitchen window. These were flowers with special powers. When Papa moaned about a sore tooth, Mama made him chew on the roots of this flower and the pain went away; and the previous spring, when a rattlesnake bit Mr. LeBlanc while he was repairing a broken fence in his pasture, Mama created a poultice using the same flower and saved his life. I longed to skip and play and follow the butterfly.

"He stole from me," Papa's voice cracked, as he handed over the gun. He cleared his throat. "You even charged him." Papa sounded frustrated.

The sheriff tucked the gun inside the belt at his waist. "And let him go," he replied, with a smirk, then furrowed his brow and spat onto the dusty ground. "I'm dealin' with crimes more serious than stealin' a few carrots or apples."

The other men guffawed at the sheriff's remark. I scowled at them. Mama said that stealing was a sin, no matter what. I was even sent to my room for stealing the last piece of my brother

Harold's Christmas candy and was told that Santa might not visit me next year.

"Like folks aidin' runaways," the sheriff growled, loudly. "And murder."

I braced myself. Papa was quick-tempered. Mama told us kids that we shouldn't raise our voices at him or talk back. But Alex did sometimes, and he and Papa had some awfully loud rows. Mama said that this was because Alex was almost a grown-up.

But Papa remained silent. His face was flushed but showed little emotion. Then he exhaled and replied in a tight voice, "He was stealing from me."

"Doesn't matter." The sheriff motioned to a member of the posse, who rode forward, leading an extra horse that was already saddled. "You're under arrest."

And the sheriff took Papa away.

I looked from Mama to the boys. Mama wept into the tea towel in her hands, and the boys looked angry, but they didn't move. Feeling as if I had to do something, I leapt off the porch and ran as fast as I could after the men as they trotted their horses away.

"Papa!" I cried.

But they didn't stop. And soon, he disappeared in a cloud of dust. I dropped to the ground and watched the yellow butterfly flit past my shoulder.

Please don't go.

The next day, Uncle Henri visited Papa in his jail cell in Sidney before riding out to the farm.

"They've charged him with murder," Uncle Henri told Mama, removing his hat and sitting down at the table.

Uncle Henri was Papa's oldest friend. They'd left Canada together during the rebellion in 1836 and worked as private fur trappers and traders on the Missouri River, from Fort Lookout,

South Dakota, to St. Joseph, Missouri. On one of his travels, Papa met Mama and they'd married. Soon afterward, Uncle Henri married Mama's sister, Émelie.

Mama sliced a peeled potato in half, then dropped the two halves into the large pot of water that sat on the kitchen table in front of her.

"Finish the potatoes," she told me, quietly.

I glanced up from the potato I was peeling and nodded, then turned to Uncle Henri.

"When will Papa come home?" I asked.

Uncle Henri shrugged and shook his head.

"The sheriff knows that he was aidin' the slaves," he said, as he stretched out his legs and crossed them at the ankle.

"But Picard was stealing from us!" Mama cried, angrily. "Blackmailing us!"

Uncle Henri nodded. "But this is probably a warning to other folk."

"What will happen to us?" Mama whispered, tears filling her eyes, her voice sounding brittle and perspiration beading on her pale brow.

I dropped the paring knife and jumped down from my stool, but Uncle Henri was already on his feet. He grabbed Mama's arm and led her to a chair.

Life changed for all of us at the farm. Mama always seemed to be in bed, while the boys and I attempted to keep the farm running. Charlie hauled water from a spring near the base of the hills, balancing a wooden yoke across his thin shoulders. He trudged back and forth with wooden buckets swinging, the water sloshing onto the ground and his shoes. Alex and Harold looked after the animals. They were the oldest and the best riders. Riding out at dawn each day, they patched fences, inspected water holes, and searched for lost calves. Edouard gathered and chopped firewood, then collected buffalo chips for the stove and fireplace. And I fed the chickens and gathered the eggs.

Mama had a small flock of black hens that laid large, light-brown eggs. They lived in a chicken coop that Papa had built near the side of the barn. The coop was filled with laying boxes, feeders, and roosts, and was attached to a long run. Every morning, I unlatched the door to the run, allowing the hens out into the fresh air where they ran in the grass, scratched for bugs, and basked in the sun. Then I collected eggs from the laying boxes, tidied up after the birds, and topped up their food. And every night, I'd lock the hens safely into their coop.

The hens became my companions. I'd sit on the ground in their run, and they'd jump up onto my knees, allowing me to gently pet their backs, especially one hen that I named Grace. She'd run up to me, sit down on the ground, and wait for me to scratch her neck. Each afternoon, I'd watch her seek out a warm, dry spot in the run, rake the dirt loose with her beak, then throw it up over her feathers, clucking contentedly. Once she finished her sunbath, she'd shake out her feathers, creating little clouds of dust.

But some of the other chores proved more difficult. The older boys washed the clothes in the creek, while I helped the younger ones weed the garden, but none of us really knew how to cook.

"Let's bake a pie!" I said to Mama, a few weeks later, as she was lying in bed.

She shook her head.

"Not now."

She rolled over to face the bedroom wall, placing her hand protectively over her swollen belly.

Mama no longer reminded me to wash my face or scrub behind my ears before bed, or to put on a clean frock each morning. My waist-length black hair became so matted that I was no longer able to run a brush through the back of it. Mama didn't even notice.

Each night, I'd sit on her bed and tell her stories about Grace or how the vegetables and flowers were growing, or about a new plant that I'd spotted growing on the bluff. But she'd just stare at me, her pretty brown eyes vacant and the area below them smudged with dark circles.

Then late one night, the front door of the house flew open and immediately slammed shut, waking everyone.

Mama shrieked. I jumped out of bed and ran across the hall to the safety of her bed. Alex stood bravely in the hallway, pointing Papa's shotgun into the darkness, down the stairs, while Harold stood behind him holding a lantern. The younger boys ran to Mama's room and climbed onto the bed beside us.

"Who's there?" Alex called out, his voice echoing off the wall of the dark staircase.

I pressed up against Mama's warmth in the bed. There was a shuffling sound in the kitchen at the bottom of the stairs.

"Papa?" Alex asked.

"Yes," a voice answered, hoarsely.

I leapt out of bed and ran to the hallway to stand beside Alex. Papa looked dishevelled. His hair stood out at odd angles from his head, and his normally clean-shaven cheeks were covered in whiskers. He was breathing heavily, as though winded from a long run.

I raced down the stairs and leapt into his arms.

"Papa!"

He squeezed me lightly, then set me down.

"Pack up the wagon!" Papa ordered, climbing the stairs to Mama's bedroom.

I raced after him.

Mama stood beside the bed, drawing her sweater about her shoulders.

"The trial wouldn't have been fair, Magali," said Papa, as he vehemently shook his head.

Mama grabbed the bedframe to steady herself.

"How'd you escape?" Alex asked, leaning against the doorframe.

"Burned a hole," Papa said, breathlessly. "In the floor."

Alex stared at him, his eyes filled with admiration.

"Using what?"

"The coals they gave me to heat my cell," Papa replied.

"Oh, Peter," Mama hushed.

But Papa ignored her.

"It was built up on posts. I crawled out."

Papa and the boys packed up the wagon with supplies, clothing, blankets, and food items that were close at hand. When everything was ready, I scrambled into the back of the wagon behind Mama, catching my breath.

"Who'll look after Grace?" I asked her, anxiously.

She shook her head and closed her eyes.

I tugged on Alex's sleeve.

"What about Grace?"

"Not now," he replied, pulling his arm away.

I stood up in the wagon and began moving toward the back of it.

"Sit down, Julia!" Papa snapped.

I sat back down.

"Yaw!" Papa yelled, snapping the reins sharply on the horses' backs.

The horses lurched forward, galloping away from the farm. We travelled west, crossing the Missouri River by ferry and onto the Nemaha Indian Reservation that bordered the Missouri River on its eastern face, extending ten miles to the west. It was land set aside for the mixed-race, and Mama said that we were part of that, because her mama was Oglala Sioux and her papa was French Canadian.

"We're almost there," Papa called over his shoulder to Mama, who'd been moaning in discomfort as the ruts in the trail jostled the wagon back and forth.

She pulled herself up to a sitting position and shouted and waved.

"Hello!"

We were approaching an encampment of tipis. Smoke rose slowly from the darkened flaps at the tops of the dwellings and women were tending fires and cooking outside. Children ran around, chasing one another, and boys Alex's age stood guard, watching our passage towards the encampment.

Once we'd stopped, women crowded around the wagon. These were Mama's sisters. They embraced her, then linked their arms under Mama's shoulders and walked her away towards one of the tipis. I scrambled out of the wagon and grabbed hold of Mama's skirt, following closely behind.

"No child," one of my aunts told me, pulling my hand away from the material.

I stopped in my tracks and frowned up at her.

That's my mama.

The full moon looked like a giant white ball rising above the horizon. Even though it was night, the prairie was cast in a day-like glow. Papa paced back and forth in front of the tipi where Mama lay moaning. She cried out, and I jumped up from where I sat holding the doll Mama had made me for my birthday. I pulled back the leather flap to the tipi, but was stopped by Aunt Émelie. She gently pushed me away from the opening.

"You'll see her once the baby's born," she said, softly.

I sat back down on a blanket that was folded on the ground near the tipi's entrance and stared toward the distant hills.

"Papa," I said, pointing to a figure on a horse, riding towards the camp. "Look."

Papa drew his gun from the belt at his waist, but then slowly returned it.

"It's Henri," he murmured.

The horse broke to a trot, then to a walk, before Uncle Henri dismounted.

"They're looking for you," he called to Papa.

Papa stopped pacing and walked toward him.

"Did you sell the cattle?" Papa asked.

Uncle Henri nodded.

"Horses too," he said, handing Papa some money. "Good thing too."

"What do you mean?" asked Papa.

"Your farm's for sale."

"What?" Papa exclaimed.

"He's seized it."

"Who has?"

"The sheriff," Uncle Henri explained. "He's selling it at his sale."

"He can't do that!" Papa roared.

"It's in the paper."

Uncle Henri pulled a copy of the newspaper from the pouch of his saddlebag and opened the paper to one of the pages. He then passed it to Papa, who quickly scanned the text.

"The proceeds will pay outstanding attorney's fees!" Papa read, then thumped the notice with the back of his hand. "I never had an attorney! I'm going back!"

"No, Peter," said Uncle Henri, looking Papa in the eye. "He's got a posse searching for you."

Papa kicked at the dirt with his boot and walked back toward the tipi.

I hopped up from where I sat and ran to Uncle Henri, who was tucking the folded paper back into his saddlebag.

"What about Grace?" I asked, tugging on his sleeve.

"Who's Grace?" Uncle Henri asked, frowning.

"My hen."

He paused before replying. "A fox got the hens, child."

I stared at him.

"It got into the coop," he explained, smiling softly. "Got 'em all."

I felt tears prick my eyes.

"Wasn't it locked?"

"The coop?"

I nodded.

"Nah, I left the door open."

I sank to my knees.

Oh, poor Grace.

CHAPTER 3

Papa leapt down from the seat of the wagon.

"He pointed a gun at me," he said, as he hurried towards Mama, who sat rocking Victoria, my new baby sister, in her cradleboard.

A week before the sheriff's sale, Papa had returned to the farm in Iowa to retrieve some of the possessions that we'd left behind during our hasty departure.

"Watch your sister," Mama told me quietly, rising to her feet.

I nodded and sat down. Sometimes Mama hung the cradleboard from a tree, propped it up on the ground like a chair, or carried it on her back. Beads adorning its buckskin flaps were arranged into tiny flowers. When the flaps were wrapped snuggly around Victoria, it looked as if she were swaddled in an armful of flowers. I imagined the yellow and black butterfly landing on one of the beaded flowers and fanning its wings slowly open and closed while Victoria slept.

"Who did?" Mama asked coolly, wrapping the blanket around her shoulders and folding her arms across her chest.

"A man!" he replied, waving his hands excitedly. "At the farm! He was part of the posse and said that he'd turn me in."

"Henri warned you," she said, pursing her lips together until they formed a flat line. "He told you that they were searching for you."

Papa waved his hand dismissively. "He pointed a gun at me, but I knocked it out of his hand." Papa's hand lifted into the air as he remembered.

Mama squeezed her eyes shut and pinched the bridge of her nose.

"I dove for it," Papa continued. "Grabbed it, then pointed it back at him."

His brow was deeply furrowed, and he stared at Mama, his eyes wild. "It fired, Magali."

"No!" she exclaimed, opening her eyes wide. "He's dead?"

Papa shrugged.

"Peter," she gasped. "No!"

"We gotta leave," he told her, burying his fingers in his hair. "They're gonna find me."

Mama's eyes filled with tears. She blinked rapidly, trying to hold them at bay, but they spilled out between her eyelids. She wiped at them impatiently with her sleeve and hurried off toward the creek in the direction of my aunts' voices.

Papa stuffed his hands into his pockets and kicked at the dirt.

"I was just defending myself," he muttered, then slowly walked back to the wagon.

I was left rocking Victoria in her cradleboard.

Papa insisted on leaving immediately, but Mama refused. She said that Victoria was still too small to travel, and we couldn't chance the weather turning and winter setting in. So, the following spring, once the drab prairie landscape was dotted with mauve cup-shaped crocuses, and the streambeds were swollen with runoff from the melting snow, we departed. We travelled north towards the confluence of Plum Creek and Bad River, where Grandmother lived.

Mama and Papa all but forgot about me after we arrived. Mama was bedridden again with a difficult pregnancy, and the older girls in the camp took over caring for Victoria.

"Leave her be," a tall girl scolded me, when I picked up a sobbing Victoria, before taking my sister from my arms.

"She's my sister," I retorted, stomping my foot.

"You're too young to help," said the girl, smirking.

I ran to Mama. She was lying in bed and staring vacantly.

"Mama!" I whined. "They won't let me help with Victoria!"

Her eyes briefly focused on me, then closed, and she rolled to face away from me. I ran outside and spotted Papa walking towards the bluff.

"Papa!"

I ran to catch up with him and grabbed hold of his hand. He pulled it away.

"Not now, Julia," he said, impatiently, then continued walking.

"But Papa," I cried, catching up with him and tugging on his sleeve. "They won't let me help with Victoria."

He stopped walking and glared at me. I'd seen this expression before, when he'd discovered the boys sledding down the snow-covered hills, instead of doing their chores. I remembered how his face turned bright red and his temper boiled over. I stopped in my tracks, dropped my hand, and didn't say another word. Papa turned and walked away.

I wandered over to where my brothers were playing with the other boys from camp. They were all standing in a circle surrounding one of the boys. Each of the boys in the outer circle stood on a blanket and changed places with each other. They jumped from blanket to blanket while the boy in the middle tried to claim one of the vacated spots.

I watched and waited. When I spotted an empty blanket, I leapt forward to claim it and smiled.

"Julia!" Alex scolded, picking himself up from the grass beside the blanket, where he'd fallen in order to avoid landing on me. "Go away! Girls can't play this!"

I stared up at him, and at the angry faces of the other boys who'd crowded around him, and felt my face become hot. I turned and ran, racing away until my lungs burned and I could run no farther, then dropped to the ground and rolled onto my back, trying to catch my breath. I stared up at the pale blue sky. A hawk soared high overhead, scanning the ground for the movement of small rodents. Its mouth opened, emitting a high, piercing scream while it circled over the landscape, gliding silently without flapping its wings. The sunlight shone through its wing and tail feathers.

A shadow then fell over me. I shaded my eyes and squinted upwards. It was Grandmother.

"Hello," she said, warmly, her soft brown eyes crinkling at the corners as she smiled.

She held out her hand. I grabbed it, and she pulled me to my feet and against her into a hug. She felt warm and safe, and she didn't let go. Instead, she rocked me gently, stroking my hair until I felt the tension in my body draining away, and I began to sob.

When my sobs turned to hiccups, she knelt down and faced me.

"What's the matter?" she asked softly, drying the tears on my cheeks.

I shrugged but didn't say anything. She raised her eyebrows, waiting for a reply.

"No one wants me," I said, as my body shuddered with a hiccup.

"Hmm. That's not true," she told me, matter-of-factly. "I do."

I stared at her and felt a lump form in my throat.

"But Mama and Papa don't," I whispered. I'd always spent time with them, but lately, things were different.

Grandmother sighed. "This is a tough time for them."

"Why?"

"They feel like they've lost everything."

I stared at her.

"They have?" I asked.

She nodded. "Their farm and their livelihood. And hope."

"Hope?"

She nodded. "Mama's worried about their future. And what will happen to your family." She paused for a moment, and then continued. "And she's angry at your papa."

"At Papa?"

"She thinks that none of this should have happened," she added. "But your papa feels that none of this was his fault."

I frowned, not understanding what she was telling me. "But why did the boys tell me to go away?"

"Oh, they're just being boys." She drew me into another hug.

Grandmother and I walked along the grassy banks of the creek, edged with shallow water, toward a grove of cottonwood trees. Dragonflies swooped along the surface of the water, and the whine of mosquitoes resonated above the sound of water trickling around the rocks in the creek. She'd taken me under her wing and was kind and patient, but strict too. She told me that I needed to keep busy and was determined to teach me quillwork.

I pointed to a path of teardrop-shaped prints along the muddy bank. "Deer!"

Grandmother was teaching me how to identify animal tracks and made a game of it as we walked.

She smiled and nodded, then pointed to another set of tracks. "What's this one?"

I knelt down and peered at the footprint. It was shaped like an egg with four toe prints and nail marks above it. It was right behind the deer tracks. I ran my fingers over the damp mud.

"Coyote?"

She nodded. "It was probably hunting the deer."

When we reached the trees, Grandmother pointed to strips of missing bark partway up the trunk on one of the trees.

"What happened?" I asked.

"A porcupine stripped the bark. They chew through the outer layer and eat the soft inner bark."

"No," I said, laughing, then glanced at Grandmother, who looked serious. "But how could it reach?"

"They have very sharp nails and are good at climbing," she said, pointing to a hollow below the exposed roots of a tree at the bank. "And this is where one lives."

She found a long stick and began poking it into the hollow. She didn't stop until the porcupine was rooted out of its den. It scurried out toward her, quills first, trying to drive its tail against her and making a chattering sound. I jumped behind her, but Grandmother didn't flinch. With a quick motion, she threw a blanket over the unsuspecting animal, then equally as fast, pulled the blanket back from it. The porcupine waddled away, its feet pointed slightly inward. Grandmother held up the blanket, which was covered with white quills with black tips, and smiled.

"How'd you do that?" I asked.

She removed a quill and held it up for me to see.

"Each quill has a hook," she replied.

She then showed me how to remove the quills and wash them with soap in the creek. She placed the clean quills into pots of red, yellow, and black liquid and began to heat the pots over the fire.

"The red is from buffalo berries," she explained, "yellow from sunflower petals and cattail roots, and black from grapes."

I stared at the bright colours in the pots and stirred the quills with a long stick. Slowly, the colour seeped into the tubes, turning them deep shades of red, yellow, and black. Grandmother removed them and spread them out to dry. She rummaged through her pocket bag, which hung from the belt at her waist, and took out several strands of rawhide.

"We'll start by wrapping these," she explained, placing several quills into her mouth, and resting them between her teeth and her cheek, with the barbs pointing outwards.

"What are you doing?" I asked, frowning.

"First, you have to soften the quills," she explained.

She pulled one of the quills through her teeth, flattening it, and while it was still moist, began wrapping the quill around the length of the rawhide. When she reached the end of the first quill, she pulled another softened quill from her mouth, flattened it, and wrapped it around the rawhide.

"There," she said, holding up the finished strand of rawhide.

I smiled. It was beautiful.

"Can I try?"

She nodded and handed me a piece of rawhide.

I placed a quill into my mouth to soften it, then pulled it through my teeth, just like Grandmother had done.

"Ow!" I cried, as it hurt my teeth.

Grandmother smiled.

"Use this," she suggested, handing me a bone tool and showing me how to flatten the quill.

She then helped me bend the end of the quill and begin wrapping it down the length of the rawhide.

"Did you know that porcupines haven't always had quills?" she asked.

"They haven't?"

"No, not always. Didn't your mama ever tell you this story?"

I shook my head.

"A long time ago, Porcupine was in the woods, and Bear tried to eat him. But Porcupine climbed a tree to safety. When he climbed down, the tree's thorns pricked him. It was a hawthorn tree."

"Alex picked his finger on a thorn," I said, looking up at Grandmother. "It swelled and turned red."

She nodded and smiled.

"This gave Porcupine an idea. He broke off some of the hawthorn branches and put them onto his back. Later, when Bear wandered back into the woods, he spotted Porcupine and pounced on him. Bear was pricked by the thorns and ran away. Iktomi watched this and asked Porcupine how he had scared Bear away."

"Who's Iktomi?"

"A spirit," she replied. "Porcupine explained that he was always in danger around Bear and showed Iktomi the hawthorn branch. Iktomi took some hawthorn branches and peeled off the bark until it was white, then put some clay on Porcupine's back and stuck the thorns into the clay. He made it part of Porcupine's skin, then told Porcupine to go back into the woods."

I was fascinated by the story as Grandmother continued.

"Soon, Wolf spotted Porcupine in the woods and sprang on him. He howled as the thorns on Porcupine's back pricked him, and he ran away. Then Bear came along, but spotting the thorns on Porcupine's back, he was afraid and wouldn't go near Porcupine. And that's why porcupines have quills today."

Quillwork soon became my passion. I practiced every day, with Grandmother looking on and encouraging me. She taught me how to plait and twist the quills, and how to create stitches on the rawhide. One day, Grandmother handed me a folded piece of buckskin.

"This is for you," she said, smiling.

It was a pocket bag just like hers.

"You can keep your sewing materials in it. And I'll help you decorate it with quillwork."

I looked up at her, my eyes welling with tears.

"It's called the Homestead Act," said Uncle Henri.

He'd come for a visit, bringing the latest news on the Civil War that was raging in the east. He also spoke about the tensions mounting between the US Army and the Indians.

"What's it for?" Papa asked.

"They're opening up settlement in the west," Uncle Henri explained, striking a match and lighting a cigarette.

"But what does it mean?" Papa repeated, raising his eyebrows and staring pointedly at Uncle Henri.

I looked up from my quillwork. Papa sounded impatient, but Uncle Henri wasn't bothered by this. Instead, he smiled, pulling deeply on his cigarette and then exhaling slowly before answering Papa.

"It means that the head of a family can claim one hundred and sixty acres of federal land."

"What's the price?" said Papa, sceptically.

"There's a filing fee," Uncle Henri replied. "And you have to live on the land for five years."

"Five years?"

Uncle Henri nodded.

"Did you hear that, Magali?" said Papa, enthusiastically. "Five years!"

He began pacing back and forth with his hands joined behind his back, looking animated and younger, like he'd been back in Iowa. I glanced at Mama. She held Victoria in her arms and stared blankly at Papa before walking away.

Papa wasn't deterred. He spent hours talking to Uncle Henri and became obsessed with the idea of heading west.

"We can own a farm again!" Papa told Mama later, rubbing his hands together.

"But where?" she asked, flatly.

"Oregon, or California," he suggested. "We'll stop when we find good land. It's our chance to make a fresh start."

Mama pursed her lips.

"How long would this trip take?" she asked, folding her arms across her chest.

"If we left next spring, after the baby's born, we'd be there by winter."

Mama grimaced and clutched at her belly. I jumped up from where I sat on a pile of bison hides playing with Victoria and ran to Mama on the other side of the tipi.

She waved me away.

"I'll be okay."

I sat down beside her and frowned at Papa. I didn't want to leave Grandmother.

"But Peter, how could we manage?" Mama asked. "We'd need food and supplies."

He nodded enthusiastically.

"We'd prepare the wagon over the winter."

"But Peter," said Mama, as she shook her head slightly. "We couldn't possibly bring enough food. The boys are always hungry."

Papa turned his face away and didn't answer.

"Peter?" Mama frowned.

He glanced at her, then looked away, his breath quickening. Then he swallowed hard.

"Peter!" said Mama, sounding alarmed. "What is it?"

"We wouldn't take them," Papa answered, his eyes averted.

I stifled a cry with my hands.

CHAPTER 4

"Mama!" Charlie screamed, struggling to free himself from Alex and Harold's hands, which firmly gripped his shoulders.

"Don't leave us!" Edouard sobbed, as Grandmother held him tightly against her.

I stared at them, and then at Grandmother. She raised a hand to me and smiled her lovely smile.

A bee buzzed past me, landing on the bright yellow centre of a crocus's mauve petals. I watched the bee flit from flower to flower until tears blurred my vision, then felt for the pocket bag at my waist, running my fingers over the quillwork design that partially adorned the outside of it. Grandmother had filled it with a supply of quills, rawhide, and my quill-flattening tool. A lump formed in my throat, and I swallowed hard.

Mama sat under the roof of white canvas, which was stretched over the ribs of the wagon, staring straight ahead. She'd hugged each boy in turn, told them that she loved them, and then walked away without looking back. Tears streamed down her cheeks as she climbed into the back of the wagon, oblivious to Victoria's cries from where she was nestled on the top of a soft pile of quilts in the back of the wagon, and ignoring baby Joseph's wails from the cradleboard that rested near her feet. I picked up Joseph's cradleboard and rocked him gently. He was the newest addition to our family and had been born at the end of the previous summer.

"Getup!" Papa commanded his team sharply, seemingly indifferent to the state of emotions around him.

Wil, the lead ox, whose rusty red shoulders were as tall as Papa's, stepped forward. Following his cue, and feeling the tug on the wooden yoke securing the two oxen's necks together, Thom stepped forward too. The heavily laden wagon moaned and creaked as it began moving.

We headed west and joined throngs of other travellers also making the journey, forming a wagon train. A former fur trapper, who was familiar with the route, guided the train. He decided where to cross the rivers and the distance to be travelled each day to the next watering hole. We made steady progress for the first few weeks, travelling long distances each day. The grass was plentiful and the water fresh for the wagon train's livestock, but then it began to rain. We soon learned that, when it rained, the wagon train didn't travel.

"We've gotta travel today," Papa told Mama, peering up at the dark clouds looming in the distance. "We've lost too many days."

We'd been forced to stay in the same location for over a week, and Papa was getting antsy. He was worried about crossing the mountains and wanted to ensure that we made it over the passes before it snowed the following fall.

"It's going to start raining again," said Mama, shaking her head.

Papa nodded. "But we can't lose any more time."

"But no one else is traveling today."

"That's good," Papa answered, sharply.

Mama frowned.

"What do you mean?"

"There are too many people," Papa explained. "I keep looking over my shoulder."

Mama turned pale.

"We're safer travelling in a group, Peter."

"I'm better at navigating," he muttered, his brows knit tightly together and his eyes drawn into angry slits. "Plus, you've heard them. They call my children mongrels!"

I stared at Papa. I didn't know what the term "mongrel" meant, but could tell from his tone that this wasn't something good. I looked from Victoria and Joseph to the other children around us. I couldn't see any difference, except that their skin and hair were darker.

"It doesn't matter what people say," said Mama, attempting to reason with him. "We know who we are."

"They call me 'squaw man'!" he spat.

"You won't listen to me, yet you listen to them," she told him, angrily.

But Papa was adamant, and we packed up the wagon.

"Ain't gonna work," one of the men sneered at Papa, as he began yoking the oxen.

"Getup!" he commanded Wil. Papa flicked the whip and the wagon creaked forward.

"You'll regret it when yer stuck in the mud," another man added, guffawing.

A storm loomed on the horizon for most of the morning and the rain was held at bay, but by noon, the cloud layer became darker and the wind picked up, bringing with it a sweet, pungent smell. Then the rain began to fall, saturating the already muddy trail and deepening its ruts.

"We should turn back," Mama called to Papa.

But he wouldn't stop. He lifted his hand dismissively and kept walking.

"Peter, you're being stubborn."

We began our descent down one of the hills on the trail. It wasn't particularly steep or long, and Wil and Thom performed well, raising their heads to brace the wagon's load against their horns, slowing the wagon's descent down the hill. The bottom of the hill was boggy, but the oxen stepped up out of the mud, beginning their ascent up the next hill. However, they soon stopped and began straining against the wooden yoke at their necks. The wagon was stuck in the hole.

"Damn it!" cursed Papa. "Getup!"

Wil and Thom struggled against the mud holding the wagon back. Papa tapped the slender stick against Wil's rump. The oxen struggled, straining against the yoke, but kept slipping on the wet hill.

"Magali!" Papa shouted. "Get everyone out of the wagon!"

"We shouldn't have travelled today," Mama sighed, loudly.

Papa walked back to the wagon.

"We gotta lighten the load."

He helped Mama, Victoria, and Joseph, in his cradleboard, out of the wagon, and I climbed out the back.

"Getup!" Papa ordered the oxen.

Wil and Thom struggled against the mud holding the wagon, but it didn't move. Papa stepped back into the bog at the bottom of the hill, sinking partway up his boots.

"Damn it!"

He pulled himself out of the mud and onto the prairie grass beside the trail. The grass was long and mixed with coarse stalks of alfalfa with yellow, purple, and blue blossoms. Papa began pulling handfuls of the stalks and stacking them into a pile. I ran to his side and joined him, tugging hard at the stalks, ignoring the pain as the blades cut the skin on my fingers.

Papa laid the grass in front of the wagon's wheels.

"Can you urge Wil forward?" he asked me. "I'll stand here and add more grass."

I nodded, picking up Papa's long whip and standing next to Wil.

"Getup!" I commanded, but he didn't budge.

"Tap him with the whip," said Papa.

"Getup!" I said more loudly, while snapping the whip on Wil's rump. "Papa, he won't move!"

Papa marched toward me and saw Wil tilting his horns at me.

"Oh no, you don't!" Papa roared.

He stood in front of Wil and looked him in the eyes. Wil stared back with his ears pricked forward. They stared at each other for a few minutes, neither backing down. Papa growled, and finally Wil put his ears back.

"What happened?" I asked, frowning.

"He was arguing with me!" replied Papa. "Okay, try again."

"Getup!" I told Wil, flicking his rump with the whip.

Wil and Thom began to move forward, straining against the yokes. The wagon wheels gained some traction on the grass and the front wheels moved slightly up and out of the hole.

"Get them to stop. I'll add some more grass," Papa called.

"Whoa!" I commanded.

Wil stopped, and Thom followed suit. Papa placed more grass in front of the wheels, then asked me to get the oxen to move forward again.

"Getup!" I ordered, snapping the whip against Wil's rump.

Again, the oxen moved the wagon a little further out of the hole. Slowly, we worked together, urging the oxen out of the hole, adding more grass for traction, and up the next hill. But when we got to the top, Thom was limping.

"What happened to him?" I asked.

"He's thrown a shoe," replied Papa.

Once we'd found a suitable location to stop for the night, Papa put a rope around Thom's girth behind his withers, and added another at his flank. Papa then began tightening the ropes. Thom's knees began to buckle, and he slowly dropped to the ground and rolled onto his side.

"Thom!" I cried out, running towards him.

"No, Julia," said Papa, catching me with his arm. "He might kick you."

Papa tied Thom's feet with a rope.

"Doesn't that hurt him?" I asked.

Papa shook his head. He set a shoe on one side of Thom's cloven hoof and hammered nails through the holes of the shoe and up through the wall of Thom's foot, securing it. He clipped the tips of the nails so that they lay flush with the outside of Thom's hoof, before attaching another shoe to the other half of Thom's hoof.

The rest of the month was rainy. On some days, the sky became very dark, and the rain fell in sheets that soaked the canvas covering the wagon. At other times, the rain was mixed with ice that hurt my head and back when it came down. The thunder would sometimes boom so loudly during the night that Victoria and Joseph would start screaming as the dark sky was cut in half by bright bolts of lightning. Some nights, I'd lie awake on the mattress in the wagon, watching its bright flashes on the horizon.

And then the month changed to July, and the tap turned off. The trails dried up, becoming so dusty that we had to cover our noses and mouths in order to avoid breathing in the dust.

"Papa!" I called, through the scarf that covered my mouth. "Something's wrong with Thom!"

"Whoa!" Papa commanded.

He walked over to where I stood next to Thom, who was sticking out his tongue and panting.

"He's overheating," said Papa, examining Thom's nostrils. "It's the dust. He can't cool off."

He took a rag out of his pocket and cleared the coating of dust from Thom's nostrils. He then handed the rag to me.

"Keep his nose clear; otherwise he'll die."

Papa opened the barrel of water at the back of the wagon and filled a small bucket. He offered Thom a drink before pouring the remaining water over the animal's back.

"That should help him until we find water."

We walked for several more hours until we came to a small bluff, where there was a stream at the bottom of the ravine. Papa unyoked Thom and led him to the sun-dappled, rippling water. Thom took a long drink, and I helped spray his sides with cool water.

"It's too hot to travel any more today," Papa told Mama, wiping the back of his neck with a cold, wet rag.

"We need to get to the trees," Mama replied, pointing to a thicket of trees in the distance.

"He won't make it. It's too hot."

"But we can't camp here," said Mama, raising her voice as she looked at the surrounding barren expanse. "This isn't a safe place to camp. It's too open. It isn't far to those trees."

"He's overheated," said Papa, frowning as he looked at Thom, who lay on the ground. "We'd risk losing him. And then how would we travel?"

"But we're too exposed here," Mama insisted, pressing her lips together before turning away.

CHAPTER 5

A hand clamped down over my mouth, pinning me to the pillow. I struggled to move out from under the hand, but the harder I fought, the tighter the grip became, each finger digging painfully into my cheekbone. I stared into fierce, wild eyes. The campfire flames outside the wagon cast eerie shapes that moved across the canvas, illuminating the streaks of black paint on the man's face. Panic gripped me. I struggled harder, grabbing his wrist with my hands and pushing upwards, but he quickly displaced my hands. He pinned them to the mattress with his free hand, and then glared—a look that seared through me. I stopped fighting but remained taut and tense.

Sensing my defeat, the man removed his hand. I gulped at the fresh air but was immediately repulsed by the rank smell of sweat that had invaded the inner sanctity of the wagon where I slept. I scrambled forward in the wagon. It was a warm night and the wagon's cover was only partially closed, allowing a breeze to drift through while I slept. The man grabbed my leg and began pulling me toward the back of the wagon. I kicked and twisted and began screaming, trying to break free from his grasp, but he was too strong and dragged me out of the wagon. The man picked me up, threw me onto his shoulder, and began running toward the trees.

I heard Mama screaming. Victoria and baby Joseph slept with her in a tent set up on the ground outside the wagon. Papa's bedroll was set up under the wagon.

"Mama! Mama!" I yelled.

"Julia!"

I pushed myself up from the man's shoulder and peered back at the camp. I caught my breath as I watched Mama crumple to the ground, and saw the dark shadow of a man standing over her with his arm raised, as though ready to strike.

"Papa!" I frantically scanned my surroundings for my father but couldn't see him anywhere.

I heard Victoria screaming my name and turned in the direction of her voice, seeing two fierce-looking men with streaks of black paint on their faces. One was carrying Victoria, and the other held Joseph in his cradleboard, as they hurried toward the bluff. Victoria was screaming, calling for me with outstretched arms.

"Victoria!" I cried.

I struggled to free myself, but the man only held me tighter.

"No!" I sobbed.

The man carried me into the woods, where the glow of the moon was soon extinguished by a heavy growth of trees, the light only occasionally reappearing through small clearings. The darkness felt like a heavy drape enveloping and disorienting me, deadening my senses. The only sound I heard was the man's footsteps on the undergrowth carpeting the forest floor, along with the raspy sound of his breathing as he ran. I clung to his shoulders, afraid of falling though repulsed by his warm, moist skin.

I heard the muffled sound of a horse snorting up ahead and twisted my body around to see a horse standing in the clearing. As we approached, the man stopped and lowered me unexpectedly to the ground. I lost my balance, and fell and lay still.

He grunted something that I didn't understand. I didn't move. Seemingly angered by my lack of response, the man grabbed me roughly by the arm and yanked me to my feet. I cried out, but he ignored my protests, lifting me astride the back of the horse before throwing his leg up over the horse's back behind me. Wrapping an arm around my waist, the man urged the horse forward into a canter. I gripped the horse's sides with my legs and grabbed a fistful of mane with my hands. I soon lost track of time, as the rocking motion of the horse lulled me into a semiconscious state.

Eventually, the horse stopped and my captor dismounted. Ahead of me in the clearing was an encampment. The sky was lightening with the promise of the sun's return, casting a warm glow onto the nearby tipis. I watched thin columns of smoke drift slowly upwards into the still morning air from the smoke-darkened flaps at the top of the dwellings, and saw women carrying water and wood or preparing meals. I heard the splash of water as the men walked out of the tipis towards the water's edge and leapt in.

My hopes lifted. I was at home, back with Grandmother before we'd set out in the wagon, and before our family had been torn apart and my brothers left behind. Tears filled my eyes and sobs wracked my body.

Someone grabbed my arm. I glanced down and saw that it was my captor. He pulled me down roughly from the horse. I landed in a heap on the ground by his black moccasin-covered feet. He jerked me to my feet, and marched me forward. I stumbled, and he pulled me along sharply by my arm. I winced. This wasn't home. The image of Mama's crumpled body and Victoria's outstretched arms flashed in front of my eyes, their screams echoing in my ears.

The man pushed aside the leather flap that covered the low opening, and then pushed me forward into the tipi.

I froze.

CHAPTER 6

After a long, stunned moment, I ran forward and pulled Victoria into a big hug, and then glanced around. Joseph was sound asleep in the cradleboard, which rested on a pile of bison hides. I breathed a sigh of relief.

"I want Mama," Victoria whimpered.

"So do I," I replied, soothingly.

I sat down and Victoria crawled onto my lap. She peered up at me with large, scared eyes. "Where is she?"

The image of Mama's crumpled body flashed before my eyes. I closed them briefly, trying to erase the memory.

"Probably searching for us."

"With Papa?"

I nodded.

"Will they come for us?"

"They'll come," I replied, squeezing her lightly. "Why don't you try to sleep?"

I arranged the soft hides around Victoria and lay down beside her. I began singing the lullaby that Mama sang to each of us as babies, and soon became lost in thought and drifted off to sleep.

"Mama!" I screamed sometime later, sitting up with a start.

My heart was pounding. I was disoriented. The memories of the previous night's events came flooding back, and a feeling of dread washed over me. It wasn't a dream.

Oh, Mama.

I stood up and tentatively stepped outside the tipi entrance. The bright sunshine blinded me, and I held up my hand to shield my eyes. A girl's voice startled me, and I turned around. She said something to me that I didn't understand. I shook my head slightly. The girl's light-brown hair was braided into two long plaits behind her ears, and her eyes were bright blue.

"What's your name?" she finally asked me in French.

"Julia," I answered, quietly.

She paused before replying.

"I'm Sara," she continued in French.

I nodded. The girl sat down on a blanket that was spread out on the ground just outside the entrance to the tipi, and then pointed to another close to it.

"Sit," she instructed.

I looked around. A few women were cooking over a fire and others sat talking and laughing while children skipped, played, or chased each other nearby.

"Sit," the girl repeated.

I knelt, and whispered to her, "Where am I?"

"With the Blackfoot."

I caught my breath, and then scrambled to my feet and darted towards the flap to the tipi where Victoria and Joseph slept.

"What you doing?" Sara asked, frowning.

"I have to go."

"Why?" She narrowed her eyes.

"They'll kill me." I looked looking nervously at the girl. "They'll kill us."

"Who will?"

"They will!" I said, anxiously, pointing at the women and children who were all now staring at me. "The Blackfoot."

"No," Sara said, shaking her head and pointing to the blanket. "Now, sit down."

I stared at her. "Why aren't you scared?"

"Why should I be?"

"Because they hate you!" I cried. "You aren't Blackfoot!"

"That's true. My parents were French Canadian, but they don't hate me because of this." Sara glanced over at the women cooking over the fire, then back at me. "Why do you think that they hate you?"

"Mama said so!"

Sara frowned.

"Why did she tell you that?"

"Because her family is Sioux, and the Blackfoot are enemies of the Sioux!"

Sara continued to stare at me. "Sit. Please."

I looked about me. The women were now engrossed again in their conversation. I felt confused. Finally, I knelt down but remained prepared to spring to my feet, if needed.

"They don't hate you," Sara began.

"Yes, they do," I insisted. "The Blackfoot hate the Sioux."

She shook her head and sighed.

"Maybe, but you're only a child. They don't hate children."

"Then why am I here?" I asked, confused by what she was saying.

"They'll adopt you."

"Adopt me?" I said, frowning.

She nodded.

"What does that mean?"

"They want to keep you here."

"But they hurt Mama," I said, tears filling my eyes.

Sara looked at me, and then stared at the horizon.

"They killed mine," she said, her voice sounding brittle.

"They killed your mama?"

She nodded. A look of sadness washed over her face, but she quickly shook it off. "Papa too."

"How long ago?" I asked, softly.

"When I was nine."

"How old are you now?"

"Fifteen," she replied, running her hands over the buckskin skirt covering her legs, smoothing out the skirt's wrinkles.

"Have you been here ever since?"

She nodded.

"But, why did they kill them?"

She shrugged, and frowned.

"Did anyone look for you?" I asked.

She shook her head again.

"We were on our own. It was only Mama and Papa and me. There wasn't anyone to search for me."

She pursed her lips. I stared at the children playing nearby, and then looked back at Sara.

"I don't know what happened to my papa," I said.

She reached forward and lightly squeezed my arm.

"Do you miss them?" I whispered.

She nodded and wiped at the tears in her eyes with the backs of her hands.

"But I like my new family too," she said, smiling brightly.

"Your new family?"

"Yes, they adopted me when I was brought here."

I stared at her.

"You'll be adopted too," she explained.

"No. I don't need a new family," I said, shaking my head. "I already have one."

She shrugged again.

"Julia!" Victoria screamed from inside the tipi. "Julia!"

I quickly got to my feet and ran inside.

Just as Sara had predicted, my siblings and I were adopted by Koko, a woman whose husband had been killed a short time before we'd arrived. She had a daughter named Kimi, who was almost the same age as Victoria, and a son named Machk, who was still a baby.

Koko was kind to us. She prepared our meals and helped me care for Victoria and Joseph. She also taught us the Blackfoot language, but I still pined for Mama and Papa. I'd sit and watch the horizon, hoping to catch a glimpse of the wagon pulled by Wil and Thom, with Papa walking alongside them, carrying his long whip. And if I heard a horse ride up and snort the dust out of its nostrils, I'd run to see if it was someone to take us away.

But it didn't happen.

"They're probably not coming," Sara told me one day the following fall, as I sat anxiously on a log, watching.

It was a cold day, and the wind was gusting. I scowled at her and drew the blanket tighter about my shoulders. She sat down and put her arm around me. After a moment, I leaned in toward her and began to weep quietly.

"What if they don't come?" I asked.

"You'll be okay. You've got Koko, and your brother and sister."

She pushed her shoulder into me, pushing me away slightly so that she could look into my eyes.

"And you've got me."

I smiled sadly, and wiped away the tears.

"But why haven't they come for me?"

"Maybe they couldn't," she replied, carefully.

"Couldn't?" I asked.

She shrugged and replied softly.

"Maybe they were hurt."

I caught my breath at the suggestion.

A man walked towards us. Initially, I ignored him, until I saw Sara, brushing the stray hairs away from her face and smoothing out her dress. I glanced up at him and froze. It was him! He wasn't wearing war paint, but there was no mistaking it: he was my captor.

"Hello," he said warmly to Sara.

He then shifted his eyes toward me and looked away quickly.

"Hello," Sara replied, smiling.

I jumped up from where I sat.

Sara grabbed my arm. "Julia."

I tried to pull my arm away, but she squeezed it tighter and pulled me back down to a sitting position.

"This is Aranck."

I stared.

"Aranck and I will be married in the spring."

I kept staring at her and frowned.

"Married?" I gasped.

She nodded and smiled.

Aranck bid us farewell and walked away.

"Sara!" I said in a hushed tone. "He captured me!"

She nodded.

"But marry him? How could you after what he did?"

She shrugged. "He asked me," she replied, defensively. "He's a good man, Julia."

"But he captured me!"

"Yes," she said. "But he wasn't trying to hurt you."

"But he took me from Mama and Papa!"

Tears filled my eyes, and I ran into the tipi.

How could she?

Initially, I had difficulties forgiving Sara for her decision to marry Aranck. I felt as if she were betraying me, and I refused to speak with her. When she'd walk up to join Koko and me, I'd look away from her, and soon Sara would walk away, looking dejected.

"Why are you treating Sara like this?" Koko asked one day, when we were alone.

"I'm angry at her!"

"But why?"

"Because of who she's marrying."

"Because she's marrying Aranck?" Koko asked, and then nodded, seeming to understand.

"Yes, he captured me." I cried. "How could she?"

"But he never wanted to hurt you."

I scowled.

"But he took me from Mama and Papa." I told her, adamantly.

She closed her eyes, and then opened them and looked kindly at me.

"What you went through was horrible, but we can't change the past. Sara's a good person. Remember, she's been through a lot too. She wants to be your friend. Please don't turn your back on her."

At first, I ignored what Koko told me, but found myself alone and scared.

A few weeks later, I approached Sara.

"I'm sorry, Sara," I told her, softly.

She threw her arms around me and acted as if nothing had ever come between us.

Sara and Aranck were married the following spring. Although I wasn't comfortable around Aranck, I chose to not harbour bad feelings towards him. Around the same time, I'd stopped pining for Mama and Papa. I still had a dull ache in my heart whenever

I thought about them, but I no longer stared at the horizon each day, waiting for them to come for us.

By the time of Sara's wedding, Joseph and Machk were almost two years old. They were constantly on the move, and it seemed that we were always chasing after the two boys. With each passing day, they seemed to gain mobility and speed and were soon running and chasing after each other in the great expanse. They'd run and run, and laugh and giggle, and then suddenly drop to the ground for a nap when their little legs would carry them no farther. Joseph was such a happy little boy. He'd stretch his arms up to Koko, wanting to be picked up, and nestle his head into the base of her neck for a warm hug.

And Victoria and Kimi were inseparable. They did everything together, often sitting with their arms wrapped about each other's backs, engrossed in a private conversation, or they would giggle together at a private joke that only a four-year-old would find amusing.

I visited Sara following her wedding. She settled into married life and seemed content with her choice for marriage. Within the year, she had a baby son that she named Pierre, after her father. I'd hold Pierre for Sara or would go to the creek with her to wash her laundry. She always seemed pleased to see me and would greet me with a big hug, but I felt out of place.

At other times, I'd sit and work on my quillwork. The pocket bag that Grandmother had given to me was my most sacred item. When I wasn't busy stitching, the bag was securely fastened to the belt at my waist, a piece of my past that I treasured and always carried with me.

But I grew tired of constantly being on my own. I began following Koko onto the prairie and into the groves of willow and cottonwood trees that grew near the muddy banks of the creek. I'd watch her gather plants and herbs. I kept my distance, but gradually, my curiosity got the best of me and I'd want to see what she was intently staring at or digging up. When she'd smile at me, I'd move away. Yet eventually, during these walks, she started to tell me about the land, the animals, and about the healing powers of the plants that grew there.

One afternoon, a few years after our arrival at the Blackfoot camp, I knelt by a patch of pale lavender bell-shaped flowers with delicate petals that tipped towards the soil.

"This is a harebell," Koko explained, running a finger over the delicate petals.

She dug down into the earth below the leaves and exposed part of the roots. She then cut off several of the small threads and handed them to me. I turned them over in my hands, and raised them to my nose. They smelled earthy.

"The roots can be made into a compress," Koko explained, taking the roots from me and placing them into a leather pouch that she carried at her waist. "They can be applied to a wound to stop the bleeding and reduce swelling."

A light-brown butterfly fluttered by and landed on the side of one of the flowers. It fanned its orange-tipped wings.

"They carry sleep and dreams," Koko told me as I stared at the butterfly. "That's why we decorate children's clothing and hair with butterflies made from buckskin."

"Mama grew flowers," I whispered.

Koko nodded.

"The butterflies loved the flowers that grew below the kitchen window," I added, as my eyes began to well with tears. "They'd land on them and fan their wings in the sunshine."

Koko smiled.

"I miss Mama."

"I know you do," said Koko softly, wrapping her arm lightly around my shoulders.

I stiffened and moved away to watch the other children playing in the distance. Although Koko treated all of us as if we were her own children, and Victoria and Joseph thought of her as their mother, I resented her. I didn't want a new mother. I already had one.

Koko also began teaching me how to administer medicines. One day, a young boy about two years old was carried into our tipi by his mother.

"Sara!"

I jumped up and ran towards her. "What's wrong with Pierre?" I asked.

I peered down at the listless little boy in her arms. Normally, Pierre tried to run after Joseph and Machk, but with the three-year age difference, he couldn't keep up.

She stared down at him. "I don't know," she cried.

"It's okay," said Koko, spreading out a buffalo robe. "Lie him on the bed."

Sara placed the little boy onto the blanket and stood back, wringing her hands. He appeared listless. Koko knelt near him, placing her hand on his forehead and on the back of his neck.

"Put your hand on his forehead," she told me.

I nodded, and watched him begin to tremble as small bumps formed on his skin.

"Feel how hot and dry his skin feels?" said Koko. "He has a fever."

She removed the young boy's outer layer of clothing, and took some willow-tree root bark from her leather pouch.

"This is from the grove of trees that grow near the creek," she explained, steeping the bark in boiling water and pouring the liquid into a cup. "It's good for sore joints and even for a sore head."

When the liquid was cool, Koko fed the boy the tea. He grimaced at the taste of the liquid, but she spoke quietly to him, coaxing him to drink it.

"We'll keep him here tonight," Koko told Sara.

"Will he be okay?" Sara sobbed.

I put my arms around her.

"I'll check on him through the night," Koko promised.

Pierre stayed in our tipi overnight. Koko fed him more tea through the night, and in the morning, I woke to the sound of laughter. I sat up and saw Joseph and Machk laughing with Pierre, who was sitting up on his blanket.

"The fever's broken," Koko told me, smiling. "Feel his forehead."

I walked over and felt Pierre's forehead, which was now cool. I smiled at Koko, and she wrapped her arm lightly around my shoulders.

"Joseph and Machk," said Koko, smiling, "run to Sara and tell her that Pierre's fever has broken."

A few days later, Koko was called to the bedside of an elderly woman in camp, and I went with her. The woman lay still on a bed of bison hides until she'd been overcome with a coughing spell that wracked her frail body, leaving her exhausted.

Koko knelt and helped the woman to a sitting position while she coughed. We learned that the woman had been ill for a few weeks and that her cough was getting progressively worse.

"What do you think?" Koko asked me.

I thought for a moment.

"Aspen tree bark?" I suggested.

"Yes," Koko smiled. "We'll make a tea."

I boiled the water and added the inner bark of the tree. Once it was steeped, Koko poured the tea into a cup and gave it to the woman to drink. The warm liquid suppressed her cough, allowing her to rest. Over the next few days, she began improving and was soon up and out of bed.

Later that month, Joseph and Machk ran into our tipi, both wailing in pain.

"What's wrong?" I asked, setting aside my quillwork and leaping to my feet.

"They stung us!" Joseph cried, holding out his arm.

There were several angry red welts along the length of it and another welt on his cheek.

"What did?" I asked.

"Wasps!" cried Joseph.

"I stepped on their nest in the ground!" Machk sobbed.

There were several red marks at the base of his neck. I picked up Grandmother's pouch, took out purple coneflower roots, and began steeping them in boiling water.

"What happened?" Koko asked, stepping into the tipi.

"We got stung!" Machk wailed.

She embraced both boys, then turned to me.

"What will you do?"

"I'm boiling coneflower roots," I explained. "I'll apply them to the stings."

Koko smiled and nodded.

"Sounds like a good idea," she said, walking out of the tipi and leaving me to care for the boys.

Soon, Koko started calling on me to gather the plants on my own. One afternoon, I walked towards a small outcrop of sandy-coloured rock. I felt the warmth of the sun on my back and watched the wind send ripples of swishing grass cascading across the prairie, while the prairie dogs sat at the mouths of their burrows, whistling as I walked past. I felt at peace and hummed to myself.

A scream shattered the stillness. It was a child's scream, and it flooded me with fear. I picked up my leather quill-covered pouch, which I'd placed onto the ground while I dug down to the roots of the strawberry plants. I drew the pouch's strap across my body, then raced back towards the camp, frantically scanning the area for Victoria and Joseph.

"Be safe," I repeated over and over as I ran. "Please, be safe."

I could see people scurrying about in the camp. A small child was being lifted and carried towards the creek that meandered a short distance away from the camp.

I spotted Victoria sitting on the ground, hugging her knees.

"Victoria!" I called.

She jumped up and ran to me.

"He's dead!" she cried.

CHAPTER 7

"Dead?" I cried. "Who's dead?"

"Joe!" Victoria whimpered.

"Stay here," I told her.

I ran to the creek, where a group of women milled about on the muddy shore. Koko was kneeling in the water, holding Joseph's limp body in her arms. She peeled the blackened, charred remains of his shirt from his small chest, allowing the water to flow over his burned skin. Joseph whimpered.

I splashed into the creek and knelt down beside Koko.

"What happened?" I whispered, tears running down my cheeks.

"The boys were playing near the fire, and Joseph fell into the flames."

I caught my breath, as the little boy's eyes closed.

"Joseph!" I screamed.

His eyes briefly fluttered open, and then closed again.

"This water's too cold for him," I yelled.

"No," said Koko, gently but firmly. "We have to stop the burning."

"Will he die?" I asked.

"No," she replied, looking directly into my eyes. "I won't let him."

I burst into tears.

"It's okay," said Koko. "But you must be strong now, Julia. I need thistle blossoms. I'll get one of the women to hold him in the water to stop his skin from continuing to burn, while I pick some thistle blossoms."

"No, you stay with him," I told her, wiping my tears on my sleeve. "I'll run and pick them."

"Okay. Do you remember the thistle plant, with the spines and pink flowers?"

"There are some by the rocks," I said, pointing south of the camp.

Koko nodded. "Go pick some blossoms. Hurry now."

I stood up, crossed the slippery stones on the creek bed, and then climbed up its muddy banks. I ran back towards the rocky outcrop where I'd spent the early afternoon. My chest burned and the sharp pain from a stitch stabbed my side, but I kept running until I'd retraced my steps back to the rocks.

I scanned the area for the pink, brush-like flowers and spotted a small dense growth of the spiny plants. I was jabbed by the prickly green leaves as I picked some of the broad blossoms, but I ignored the pain and then ran back to camp.

"I found some," I gasped to Koko.

She was still kneeling in the cold creek water, holding Joseph's limp body. She was shivering and her lips had assumed a bluish tinge, even though she now had a blanket wrapped about her shoulders, presumably from one of the women who looked on from the shore.

"Could you hold Joseph in the water?" Koko asked, her lips hardly moving and her words slowed and slurred by the cold. "While I prepare the thistles?"

I removed my leather pouch and placed it onto the creek bank, then stepped into the creek and kneeled in the icy water.

"Keep his burnt skin in the water," Koko advised, transferring Joseph to my lap.

I adjusted him in my arms, allowing the water to flow over the raw pink skin on his chest.

"This won't take long," said Koko.

She climbed stiffly out of the water, picked up my leather pouch and made her way to the tipi.

I stroked Joseph's forehead, watching the ripples of clear water flow past us and over the smooth rocks on the bottom of the streambed. The gentle breeze numbed my wet skin.

"Please, keep him safe," I repeated. I then began humming softly.

I rocked Joseph gently in the stream and laid my face against his cold cheek.

"I'll take care of you, Joseph," I promised.

"I will too," added Koko.

I looked up and Koko smiled.

"He's been in the water long enough to stop the burning. Let's put some of the thistle blossom onto his burns."

Back at camp, I changed into dry clothing, and then watched Koko apply the liquid from the boiled thistle blossoms to Joseph's burned skin.

"What does that do?" I asked.

"It will soothe his burned skin and keep it soft."

"Will he be okay?"

Koko smiled up at me.

"Yes."

"Thank you," I said, softly.

Koko hugged me gently, and I hugged her back.

The burns to Joseph's chest healed remarkably quickly, and he was soon out of bed, playing with toy arrows and spears and running across the wide-open prairie, trying to manoeuvre through the tall sea of moving grass with Machk in pursuit.

I looked at Koko differently after the accident. I saw how much she and the others cared for Joseph and was touched by this. Although I still struggled with a deep feeling of resentment about what had happened to my parents, I stopped pushing Koko away. And in return, she assumed the role of the mother that was missing in my life.

"I'm the fastest!" Joseph declared, touching my arm and pulling up sharply in front of me after a full-out sprint.

"Are not!" Machk replied with a scowl, touching my arm a close second.

"I sure am!" Joseph gloated.

Machk gave Joseph a small shove.

"Boys!" Koko called out sharply as she walked toward us.

She looked from one boy to the other, and then rolled her eyes and shook her head at me.

"Come, sit," she told the boys, pointing to the ground near where she stood. "Have you heard the story about the deer and the antelope?"

Both boys shook their heads.

"A long time ago," she began, "an antelope met a deer on the prairie. They greeted each other politely, but soon, the antelope boasted about how fast he could run, and not to be outdone, the deer bragged about how fast he could run. And in no time at all, the antelope declared that he was the fastest and could outrun the deer. Not to be outdone, the deer boasted that he could beat the antelope."

Koko looked from one boy to the other before continuing with her story.

"So, they decided to have a race to see who was the fastest, and as a wager, they bet their gall."

"What's gall?" Machk asked.

"Nerve or boldness," Koko replied. "So, they raced across the open prairie and the antelope won the race, then took the deer's gall.

"But soon, the deer grumbled that, although the antelope may have beaten him in a race on the open prairie, if they were to race through the forest where deer lived, he would most certainly win. So, he challenged the antelope to another race. Feeling confident after his win, the antelope agreed. The wager for this race was their dewclaws.

"The next race was run amongst the thick timber, brush, and fallen logs of the forest. This time the antelope ran slowly, since this setting was unnatural for him. He was afraid of running into a tree or stumbling over a fallen log, so the deer easily beat him and took his dewclaws. And ever since then, the deer has had no gall and the antelope no dewclaws."

Machk stood up.

"I'm the antelope!" he declared.

Not to be outdone, Joseph also leapt to his feet.

"Then I'm the deer!" he cried.

Koko shook her head. "You're both fast, but you also both have your own strengths," she said, looking from one boy to the other. "Joseph, you're good at running through grass that reaches to your shoulders. And Machk, you're faster when the grass isn't so high."

Joseph stuck his tongue out at Machk, and ran off, with Machk in pursuit. Koko just shook her head.

There was a commotion at the edge of the camp, where two white men rode in, leading a few horses. The men and boys in camp moved towards the newcomers, encircling them.

"Why are they here?" I asked, frowning.

"To trade horses," Koko replied.

I spotted Joseph running towards the men, and pushing to the front of the circle. Without thinking, I ran towards the group and forced my way past the men to reach him.

"No, Joseph!" I scolded, grabbing his arm. "Come away!"

"No, Julia!"

Joseph pulled his arm from my grasp, and pointed up at one of the men who'd dismounted from his horse.

"Is that what Papa looked like?"

I turned and looked at the man who was now standing a short distance from me. He was tall, wore a long moustache, and one of his eyes was squinted against the sun.

"Bonjour," he greeted me in French.

Without hesitation, I also replied in French. "Bonjour."

I was startled by my reply, as I never spoke the language at that time.

"Do you live here?" the man asked, with a slight frown.

I nodded, and turned to Joseph, who was staring at me.

"Come, Joseph!" I said in Blackfoot, grabbing hold of his arm.

"Were you speaking Papa's language?" Joseph asked as I led him away from the strangers.

I nodded.

"Wait," the man called after me.

I stopped and turned.

"What's your name?"

"Julia," I replied quietly.

CHAPTER 8

Joseph was given a pony. He was taught to care for it, feed it, and how to ride it properly. The pony was brown and white, with a mane that was half white and half black. A frizzy black fringe of hair framed the pony's face, and he had a small snippet of white on his pink muzzle. The pony was beautiful, and I was envious.

Every day, I'd race to finish my chores so that I could spend time with the pony. I'd lie on the ground staring up at him while he grazed peacefully on the green grass. Sometimes, I'd scratch him behind his ears and laugh as he tilted his head towards me and rubbed against my hand in response.

"Julia! He's mine!" Joseph would tell me crossly, as he led his pony.

"But you haven't even named him," I'd reply, haughtily.

And on other days, I'd sit stitching quills onto a pair of moccasins or the buckskin pouch that Grandmother gave me, watching the boys in the camp race their ponies across the flat prairie. Some of the boys were natural riders and displayed great balance as they sped their ponies across the wide expanse. However, others would grasp tightly to their pony's necks and nearly become unseated as their ponies loped along.

"Why can't girls race?" I asked Koko.

I placed my quillwork aside, leaning forward, resting on my elbows with my chin in my hands.

She shrugged, not looking up from the dress that she was stitching beside me.

"Because they don't have their own ponies," said Koko.

"But I want to race a pony."

She shook her head.

"But you can't."

"Why?" I asked, frowning.

"Because you don't have a pony."

"But why can't I have a pony?"

Koko frowned and looked directly at me. "Julia, you don't need one, because you won't become a warrior."

I scowled.

And my mood didn't improve. Koko tried to keep me busy by teaching me how to tan a hide following a hunt. I learned to stake the hide to the ground and scrape off the fat and meat, followed by the hair from the other side, until the entire skin was soft and clean. I learned how to rub animal fat and liver into the hide, dry it in the sun, soak it in water, roll it into a bundle to cure, and then stretch and scrape it again. I was pleased to help and was praised for my work. Yet, as I paused to stretch my aching back from scraping the hide once again, I listened to the laughter from the boys as they raced their ponies. I felt sorry for myself and longed for more.

"I need your help," Koko told me one morning.

I sighed, and followed her out toward a herd of horses grazing in the field. A jet-black horse with no white markings was standing on its own, away from the other horses. It wasn't moving or grazing, and although it nickered at us as we approached, it didn't move.

"Isn't she beautiful?" said Koko, as she gently ran her hand down the horse's face.

As I approached, the horse reached out with its muzzle and placed it near my cheek, breathing in and out. This tickled my skin. I smiled and kissed the soft skin on the side of the horse's muzzle.

"I think that her leg is broken," said Koko.

"Broken?" I exclaimed. "Oh no!"

I remembered when one of Papa's horses had stepped into a badger hole in the field and broke its leg. Papa had told me that the horse had to be destroyed as he walked out to the field with a gun.

Koko nodded. "See how she's holding it?"

She pointed to the horse's right front leg. Only the tip of her toe rested on the ground.

I bent down to look.

"There's a hole."

I pointed to a cut at the top of her leg. It wasn't bleeding, but something white was visible in the middle of the wound.

"What's that?" I asked.

"It's bone," replied Koko, peering at the wound.

She slipped a rope over the horse's nose, twisted it below its chin, and then tied the rope up behind its ears. Koko then led the horse towards a small wooden corral that had been set up closer to camp. Although it wasn't that far, the horse was unable to walk properly. She held her right leg up off the ground and hopped on her other legs. It took quite a while to cover the distance to the corral. When we finally reached it, Koko removed the horse's rope halter, and I blocked off the opening in the fence with a pole.

"You'll need to keep the cut clean," Koko explained, pushing a few strands of loose hair out of her eyes. "If the bone's visible, it's a serious wound."

"I have to keep it clean?" I asked.

Koko smiled and nodded. "You said that you wanted a horse."

"Well, yes," I said, backing away slightly. "But I've never taken care of one."

"You'll learn," she added, smiling smugly.

A horse of my own!

But my feeling of elation soon turned to dread, as I remembered Papa's words.

"But her leg's broken."

Koko nodded. "It will heal."

"But how?"

She put her arm around my shoulders and kissed my cheek softly.

"You'll help it heal."

"But Papa said that a break couldn't heal."

She shrugged. "Some breaks are bad, but I've also seen bones heal."

"Will this one heal?"

"Yes," Koko replied, smiling softly. "She may never be completely sound, but she's just young. I think that she deserves a chance; don't you?"

I nodded.

"So, I can keep her?"

"She's all yours now," said Koko. "Her owner doesn't want her. He needs a sound horse now. She was going to be destroyed when she broke it yesterday, but I stopped him."

I couldn't believe the news.

"Where do I start?" I asked.

"Well, why don't you name her," Koko suggested, bending to take a closer look at the horse's wound.

I thought for a moment.

"Grace," I decided quickly, naming the horse after my beloved hen on the farm.

"Sounds like a fine name," Koko said, smiling. "You'll need to clean out the cut. And then, once that's healed, work on mending her broken bone."

I now had a purpose, and I became busy. I boiled strawberry roots and cleansed the wound with the liquid, then applied compresses of harebell roots. The wound healed quickly, without becoming infected, but the first few days following the break were difficult for Grace, as she was unable to lie down. This meant that the muscles in her shoulders, along her back, and in her rump became very taut. I massaged them, and this seemed to offer Grace some relief. She'd respond by leaning against me, trying to transfer some of her weight onto me, which I couldn't handle.

"What do I do?" I asked Koko. "She can't lie down."

"She'll lie down," Koko reassured me.

"But how will she get back up onto her feet."

"She'll figure it out," Koko replied, confidently. "Horses don't require four legs to stand up."

I was skeptical and steadily became more worried. Then, a few days later, I spotted Grace lying down and raced towards the corral.

"Koko!" I called to her over my shoulder. "Something's wrong with Grace!"

Koko ran after me.

"Oh, Grace!" I cried.

"No, Julia," said Koko, smiling. "Listen."

I wiped away the tears that blurred my vision, and turned my head towards the corral. There were deep sighs coming from within.

"She's sleeping?" I asked.

Koko laughed and nodded, as a dog from the camp ran under the fence and into the corral towards Grace.

"No!" I cried.

I climbed the fence to chase after the dog, but stopped and stared when the dog stood over Grace's face. It began kissing her muzzle repeatedly until she stirred, and then it went on its way.

"Why'd he do that?" I asked.

"I've seen him visit Grace before. He seems to check on her."

I sat down in the corral and waited for Grace to wake and get back onto her feet. It was a bit of a struggle initially, but she eventually managed using her three good legs; and soon, she did this with ease. She began hobbling around the corral, hopping on her good front leg while dragging the broken one along behind. I was pleased but remained concerned.

"She's wearing out the front of her hoof," I told Koko.

"How do you think we can we protect it?" she asked.

I thought about this for a moment.

"Papa put shoes on the oxen to protect them when we were on the trail. Maybe we can use a shoe?"

"That's a good idea."

"But I don't know how to shoe a horse," I said, considering the problem. "Would a moccasin work?"

Koko smiled.

"It's worth a try."

I stitched together some buckskin and fitted this over Grace's foot, securing the buckskin with a strand of sinew. This seemed to work, and Grace didn't object to the shoe. However, the buckskin quickly wore out and had to be changed frequently.

One day, when I was securing a new moccasin onto Grace's foot, I heard someone behind me.

"What are you doing?" a man's voice asked me in French.

I whirled around, dropping Grace's hoof. She groaned. It was the man who'd visited the camp earlier to trade horses. I stared at him.

"Why are you covering her foot?" he asked, smiling kindly.

I hesitated before answering.

"She's broken her leg," I explained, my French still rusty. "She's dragging her hoof, and it's wearing out."

He nodded. "How'd she break it?"

I shrugged. "I think she was kicked by another horse," I said, pointing to the scar at the top of Grace's leg. "It caught her right there."

He peered at the scar and then smiled. "And she wasn't destroyed?"

"No," I told him proudly, and then frowned. "It's healing nicely, and she's just a young horse."

He nodded, and looked down at Grace's foot.

"Did you care for her yourself?"

"Yes," I replied. "And Koko helped."

"Who's Koko?"

I paused and looked towards the camp. I could see Koko talking and laughing with Victoria and Kimi.

"She's my mother," I told him, proudly.

He looked thoughtfully at me for a moment.

"Why don't you put a metal shoe on her?"

"I don't have a metal shoe," I replied.

"I could make her a shoe."

I stared at him.

"You could?"

He nodded. "I always shoe my own horses."

"But I have no way to pay for it."

He just smiled.

The next week, he returned to camp, but instead of bringing horses with him, he brought a metal horseshoe. He built a small fire beside the coral, and using tongs, held the shoe over the flames until it glowed red in the fire. Then he placed the shoe onto

Grace's foot. There was a lot of smoke and a sizzling sound like a snake as the shoe seared the bottom of her foot. But Grace didn't flinch, nor did she react to the smell of burned hoof. The smell stung my nose, and I pinched it shut.

"Are you hurting her?" I asked.

He shook his head. "No, she doesn't feel it."

He walked back and forth, between the fire and Grace, heating the metal shoe, checking the fit, and then striking the hot shoe with a hammer to shape it and checking the fit again. Once he was satisfied, he nailed the shoe to Grace's foot, just like Papa used to do with the oxen shoes. But this shoe was different. It extended upwards over the front of Grace's hoof to protect her foot as she dragged it.

"What happened to your parents?" the man asked, letting go of Grace's foot and stroking her side.

"I don't know." I paused, and bit my lip. "We were taken from them."

"Who did this?" he asked.

"They did," I replied, quietly.

"The Blackfoot?" he asked, looking concerned.

I nodded, but quickly qualified my response. "But Koko's adopted us, and now we live with her."

He nodded and smiled softly. "How long have you lived here?"

"Since I was eight."

"And how old are you now?"

"Twelve."

After he'd created the shoe for Grace, the man stopped by the camp every few months, re-shoeing her each time. I'd learned that his name was Moïse, and that he was born in Québec. He'd travelled west with two brothers, Edouard and Antoine, and when they reached Independence, Missouri, they'd gone their separate ways. Edouard travelled on to California, while Antoine left for western Oregon. Moïse was lured by the discovery of gold in eastern Oregon and Idaho Territory, and hoping to strike it rich, he joined the gold rush. However, he didn't find his fortune in gold and instead purchased a large farm in the Grande Ronde Valley in eastern Oregon, where he built a mill on his property.

"She's no longer dragging her toe on the ground," Moïse told me one day the following spring.

I nodded. Grace was now beginning to put weight onto her leg.

"She no longer needs a shoe to protect her hoof," he continued. "Will you ride her?"

"I'd like to," I said, stroking Grace's face.

Grace rubbed her face against me. She was shedding her winter coat and was itchy. I laughed as she pushed against me, nearly toppling me over.

Moïse handed me a saddle.

"I brought you this."

"I can't take this," I said, my eyes filling with tears.

"Sure, you can. You need a saddle for riding."

I took the saddle from him.

"What kind of a saddle is this?" I asked.

The saddle was little more than a shaped piece of leather with a strap.

"I use it for training my young horses," Moïse explained. "They don't seem to mind the feel of this on their back."

Moïse placed it onto Grace's back and buckled up the strap that fit under her stomach. Grace didn't move a muscle.

"Do you want to try sitting on her?" he asked.

I'd dreamed of this day, but wasn't sure if it would ever happen.

"Will her leg be strong enough?" I asked.

"I think so," he nodded. "She's carrying weight on it now. Bend your left leg."

I bent my leg, and he took hold of my knee and my leg just in front of my left foot, and lifted me up until I sat astride Grace. She moved forward slightly under my weight to stabilize her legs, but she didn't seem to have any trouble carrying me.

I leaned forward and stroked her neck.

"Good girl," I whispered.

"I think that she'll be just fine," said Moïse as he smiled at me.

By the summer, I was taking Grace for long walks. She walked with a bit of a limp, but her bone seemed to be healed, and she was strong enough to carry my weight. I loved the feeling of freedom, with the wind in my hair and warmth of the sun on my back. Some days, I'd leave early in the morning and not return until the late afternoon.

I also taught Grace to pull a travois, and when the camp began their migration during the summer months, Grace helped to carry the load. She stood patiently while the tipi poles were lashed to her side and baggage of buffalo robes piled onto her back. She quietly followed the broken column of people as they moved out over the plain, following the buffalo. The following winter, when the snow covered the ground, I taught Grace to pull a sled made from buffalo rib bones strung together.

"I want another turn!" Victoria called out to me.

She was beaming, and the cool air had coloured her cheeks a bright red.

"No, me first," Kimi called, running after Victoria.

Although they were very close in age, Kimi was a much taller eight-year-old than Victoria and liked to assert her greater height.

"I said it first!" said Victoria, scowling.

"You can both have a turn," I replied, as I stroked Grace's face.

She was such a sweet horse and didn't seem to mind pulling the sled behind her around the open prairie, filled with squealing children. This used to be my most favourite time of the year. It was December. The daylight hours were short, and it was nearly Christmas. But now, this was the time of year when I seemed to miss Mama and Papa the most, and I'd begun to dread it.

"What's wrong?" Victoria asked me, sitting down beside me in the tipi, where I sat staring into the fire.

We'd come in from sledding, and Koko had made steaming cups of tea to warm us up.

"I'm just thinking about Mama and Papa."

"Do you still miss them?" she asked.

I nodded. "Especially at this time of the year."

Koko glanced up at me and smiled softly.

"Why?" she asked.

"It's almost Christmas."

"What was Christmas like?" she asked.

"Yeah, what was it like?" Joseph added, taking a seat close to me.

"Well, Papa would go into the woods and cut down a tall tree. He'd bring it into the house and we'd decorate the tree. Then we'd sing Christmas carols around it."

"What's a Christmas carol?" Joseph asked.

"A song about Christmas."

"What did you decorate the tree with?" Victoria asked.

"Garlands."

"What's a garland?" asked Joseph.

"We'd string popcorn together on a string and make paper chains and hang those around the tree. They were almost like fancy ropes."

"What's popcorn?" he asked.

"You make popcorn by heating kernels of dried corn," I replied. "When they heat up, they open up and are white and fluffy. We'd put a thread through them."

"What did you eat?" Victoria asked.

65

"Tourtière, cakes, cookies."

"What's tourtière?" Joseph asked.

"It's a meat pie," I explained patiently. "Mama would fill it with venison and potatoes."

"Would I like it?" Joseph asked.

I nodded. "The older boys loved it. I think that you'd love it too."

Joseph smiled broadly.

"And Père Noël would visit?" Victoria asked.

I smiled. "Oh yes. He'd leave me a piece of candy and a gift."

Tears suddenly filled my eyes. Koko stood up and walked over to me, and wrapped her arms around me.

"It's okay," she said. "It's good to keep the memories alive."

The next morning, Joseph sped into the tipi and woke me. "Julia! Julia!"

He grabbed my hand and began pulling me outside. "Come!"

I went outside with him and stopped in my tracks and stared. There in front of me was a small Christmas tree, decorated with a garland of pinecones. I looked up and saw Koko standing a small distance away with tears in her eyes, her hand covering her mouth. I ran over to her and threw my arms about her neck.

"I hope that I got this right," she whispered.

"Thank you," I gasped.

"Julia!" Joseph called. "Look!"

I walked over to the tree, and underneath it saw a pair of moccasins.

"For me?" I asked, glancing back at Koko, who nodded.

"Thank you."

"Will you teach us some Christmas carols?" Joseph asked.

I nodded. This was the best Christmas ever.

CHAPTER 9

Joseph raced towards me, nearly stumbling as he skidded to a halt in front of where I sat stitching quills onto a dress.

"He's back!" he panted.

"Slow down, Joseph," I said, absently. "Who's back?"

"The man that spoke to you!"

I looked up at him. "Which man?"

"The one that speaks Papa's language. And helped you with Grace. He was asking about you!"

"Me?" I frowned, wondering why the man would be asking about me. "Joseph, were you listening when you shouldn't have been?"

His face reddened slightly. He was saved from further embarrassment by Koko's arrival.

"Joseph," said Koko, smoothing out his thick, unruly hair, "I need to speak with Julia."

"Okay, Koko," he said, taking a seat on the ground beside me.

Koko chuckled. "No, I need to speak to her alone."

Joseph frowned, and then stood up and moved a couple of steps away from me.

"Alone, Joseph!"

He exhaled and stomped away as I laughed.

Koko looked at me, pausing for a moment.

"The Frenchman's back."

"Yes, Joseph mentioned," I replied, focusing intently on my beadwork.

"He wishes to speak with you."

"Why?" I asked.

She paused again. I looked up at her and thought she looked sad, but then she smiled.

"He wants to marry you!"

"What!" I gasped. "Marry me?"

"He's offered twelve horses for your hand in marriage."

"Twelve horses!"

"Yes," said Koko, looking very serious. "He's a wealthy man."

"Then why does he want to marry me?"

I stood up and wrapped my arms protectively around my body, and then turned to her and shook my head.

"I can't."

"Why?" she asked, looking puzzled.

"I'm too young to get married!"

"You were fifteen on your last birthday."

"Yes, but that's too young for marriage."

"I was married at your age."

I stared at her. "But I don't know anything about him."

"You've spoken with him on many occasions," she pointed out. "And he helped you with Grace."

"Well, yes, but we've mostly spoken about horses."

"You have something in common, then."

"But I don't know much about him beyond that."

I was panicking. I hadn't expected to be faced by something like this.

"But you'll get to know him," said Koko as she put her arm around me. "He's French. And so are you."

I shook her head.

"I used to be," I said, and then paused, feeling as though I were somehow betraying Mama and Papa. "I mean, Papa was French and Mama part-French, but you're Blackfoot."

Koko smiled broadly. Her eyes filled with tears, and she hugged me closely.

"My French isn't very good," I continued. "I've forgotten."

"But it will come back. You've used it to speak with him."

I shook my head and blinked back tears. "He reminds me of Papa."

Koko released me from her hug and held me at arm's length, clearly struggling with her own emotions.

"And that makes you sad?" she whispered.

"I still miss them," I replied, choking back tears. "I don't want to lose you too."

"You'll never lose me," she said, hugging me again. "You're my daughter, and I'm so proud of you."

She led me into the tipi. "Come. Let's get you changed into a clean dress."

A short while later, Koko kissed my cheek lightly.

"Go," she said, directing me out of the tipi. "Talk to him. It'll be okay."

Moïse sat on the ground in front of the fire.

"Bonjour," he said, softly.

I nodded in reply.

"How are you?"

"Fine," I replied.

"And how's Grace?"

"She's doing well," I said, with a faint smile.

"Are you riding her?"

I nodded.

He cleared his throat, and looked directly at me.

"I'd like for you to be my wife."

I nodded, tears filling my eyes.

"This makes you sad?" he asked, with a puzzled expression.

I shook my head.

"Then why do you cry?"

"What will happen to Victoria and Joseph?" I asked. "I can't leave them."

He thought for a moment.

"They can move with us."

I stared at him.

"I think that you'll like my farm. I have many horses," he explained. "You can help care for them, like you have with Grace."

I smiled softly, and panicked again.

"Grace! I can't leave Grace!"

He shook his head.

"Of course not. You'll take her too."

Later, I spoke with Koko about Moïse's proposal.

"He said that Victoria and Joseph can go with us."

"He's a generous man," Koko answered, sadly. "But you'll have to give them the choice."

I explained the situation to Victoria and Joseph.

"I said yes," I told them. "He has a horse farm in Oregon."

"Where's Oregon?" Joseph asked.

"West of here," I replied.

"But what will happen to us?" Victoria whispered, her eyes wide and beginning to fill with tears. "You can't leave us."

"You'll be fine," I said, taking her hand. "You can stay here with Koko or come with me."

"But I love both of you," she said and began to cry. "I don't want to choose."

I nodded.

"I don't remember living anywhere else but here," Joseph added, looking anxious.

I put my arm around his narrow shoulders.

"And I don't remember Mama or Papa or the older boys," he continued.

Tears filled my eyes. "You were just a baby."

"I'm scared to move away," he said.

He pursed his lips and threw his arms around me, hugging me tightly.

I wore a buckskin dress to the ceremony; it was ornately decorated with quills and beads and was a gift from Koko. She also prepared a meal, although I couldn't eat. I dreaded our departure.

"You've grown into a fine young man," I told Joseph, blinking back tears. "Mama and Papa would be proud."

"Will I ever see you again?" Joseph whispered.

"I hope so," I replied, hugging him before quickly turning away.

"Goodbye, Julia," Sara told me softly, pulling me into a hug and then releasing me.

"Thank you," I replied.

She looked torn, as if she wanted to go with me, yet wanted to stay. I smiled at her, turned to Koko.

"I'll take care of him," said Koko, reassuringly.

I nodded. "Thank you."

"I love you, my daughter," she said, hugging me tightly.

"And I love you."

And then Moïse and I drove away. Victoria sat closely beside me, with tears streaming down her face. I found it difficult to breathe, and there was a sharp pain in my chest.

Why do I always have to say goodbye?

CHAPTER 10

A second wedding ceremony was held for us once we reached Oregon. It took place at the house of Remi, a childhood friend of Moïse's.

"Hello, Julia," Remi greeted us at the door, smiling broadly at Victoria and me. "Come in, come in."

I smiled shyly, and Victoria had a scared look on her face.

"Amelie, come take Victoria to your room," Remi called to his eldest daughter, who was close to Victoria's age.

Amelie ran to us and grabbed hold of Victoria's hand, pulling her toward the stairs. Victoria pulled her arm away and stared at me.

"It's okay," I told her in Blackfoot. "She's only taking you to her room."

Victoria pursed her lips and nodded.

"She can't remember her French," I told Remi, defensively.

He smiled and nodded, and tucked my hand into his bent arm and led me into the kitchen, where his wife, Martha, was creating a bouquet of wildflowers.

This was the first house that I'd been in since we'd fled our farm in Iowa when I was a small child. The rooms were filled with formal furniture. It was beautiful, but I felt claustrophobic and was afraid to move in case I bumped into something.

"Hello, Julia," said Martha, smiling.

I nervously returned the smile, and she reached out to take my hand.

"I'll leave you," said Remi with a bow, before retreating from the kitchen.

"Don't be nervous," Martha said, pulling out a chair for me.

I sat down. There was a small mirror on the wooden table. I picked it up and looked at my reflection. It had been years since I'd last seen my face in a mirror. Sometimes, I'd get a glimpse of myself in a still body of water, but most of the time, the only nearby water had been a creek that was continuously moving. Victoria and Joseph looked like Papa, and I'd always assumed that I did too. It was a shock to see how much I resembled Mama, not so much in the colouring, but in facial structure. My cheekbones were high and my face was rounder. A feeling of homesickness washed over me as I thought of her. I replaced the mirror on the table.

"You have beautiful hair," said Martha, brushing my hair up, away from my face. "It must be a shock being here."

"Yes," I nodded. "I'm not sure where I belong."

"I understand," she said, taking a seat in the chair next to me. "My family is French Canadian, and my mother was also part Mi'kmaq."

I stared at her, and she nodded.

"When I was growing up, I felt as if I didn't belong in any world."

"That's how I feel."

"Over the years, I've grown a thick skin," she continued. "And I've also learned to keep this to myself."

I was puzzled.

"Should I pretend to be something different?" I asked.

"Oh no," she said, shaking her head and squeezing my shoulders lightly. "Be proud of who you are, but be careful who you share this with. Not all people are accepting of something different."

"Moïse doesn't seem to mind that my background is mixed."

She nodded. "Moïse is a good man, but not everyone is as accepting."

A few hours later, we were married by a Justice of the Peace. Remi and Martha were our witnesses. Then we left for Moïse's farm, where a reception was held for us. It was hosted by Moïse's French Canadian neighbours and consisted of a meal, followed by a dance in one of the large barns on Moïse's farm.

The doors of the barn were flung open, inviting the cool air inside, where men and women skipped, stepped, and tapped their boots on the bare wooden floor. They also sang *chansons à répondre*, in which one person sang a line followed by everyone else singing the next line in response.

Music drifted through the valley. The melancholy, low-pitched whisper of the fiddle was carried by the wind, followed by a crescendo, the pitch becoming higher and higher, and falling back to a soft whisper before it drifted away on the waves of the wind. Then the notes became more rhythmic, like a jig, the bowing style swing that was distinctive of French Canadian music.

Moïse walked out of the barn. His cheeks were flushed, and his brown hair was slicked back off his pale brow, which never saw the rays of the sun. He inhaled the blissful scent of freshly cut hay. The weather had cooperated, and the hay was being cut field by field by the community of farmers.

He spotted me sitting in a wooden chair near the barn.

"Are you okay?" he asked, striking a match to light a cigarette, and inhaling deeply.

I nodded. A great expanse of horse fields lay in front of me. Moïse had mentioned that he raised horses, but I never expected there to be over one hundred horses on the farm. I spotted Grace in one of the fields amongst other mares and smiled. She seemed very content.

"I knew most of them back in Québec," Moïse explained, nodding toward the barn as he walked toward me. "We travelled to Oregon with them."

He rested his elbows on the hitching post near my chair and looked out over the fields, squinting an eye shut against the setting sun.

I nodded and smiled softly.

"Why'd you move west?"

He paused for a moment.

"I wasn't the oldest son."

I looked at him, not understanding.

"My family was wealthy, but all of this would have gone to Étienne, my eldest brother," Moïse explained. "I was son number four."

I nodded.

"My brothers Antoine and Edouard were in a similar situation, not being the eldest. So, we packed up and headed west to make our own fortune."

I nodded and looked back towards the horses. I felt awkward and out of place.

"Don't you like the music?"

"Yes," I said, smiling.

"And the dancing?"

He turned to the open doors and watched the whirl of people moving in unison around the wooden floor. He turned back to me, and I shrugged.

He raised an eyebrow. "Don't you like dancing?"

I shrugged again.

"Have you ever danced before?"

I shook my head. "Not like this," I replied, quietly. Sometimes at the camp, after the sun had set, we'd danced while people sang and played the drums.

Moïse tossed his cigarette onto the dirt, stomped it out with his toe, and held his hand out to me.

"Would you care to dance?" he asked, with a formal bow.

"I don't know how," I whispered, grasping his hand.

He put my hand in the bend of his arm and held it tightly against his side.

"I'll show you," he said, with a broad smile.

And we walked back into the barn.

Moïse's house was beautiful and spacious, but I felt cramped in it and ventured outside whenever I could. I'd often take my quill-work with me and find a quiet spot where I could feel the warmth of the sun on my face, fill my lungs with fresh air, and clear my mind. I'd then gaze at the beautiful rolling patchwork of fields, including hay fields, wheat fields, and green pastures dotted with thousands of horses. The valley was shut in by the Blue Mountains on all sides except the west and east, where the Grande Ronde River flowed in and out of the valley. Its banks were lined with cottonwoods, elders, and willows, and many streams flowed down from the mountain and emptied into it. I sat and listened to the meadowlark.

A loud bray shattered the silence of the early afternoon. I leapt to my feet and glanced behind me. Moïse was walking toward me, passing in front of a field of mules. He was greeted by a light-coloured mule with long ears that had its head stuck over the fence for attention.

Moïse laughed.

"Scared her, did you?" he said to the mule, stroking its fuzzy face.

I rolled my eyes and sat back down. He sat down beside me.

"Why mules?" I asked, picking up my quillwork.

The animals had short, thick heads, long ears, and thin limbs. They were in dramatic contrast to the sleek, long-legged racehorses that grazed in adjacent fields. Their brays were also abrasive compared to the whinnies of the horses.

Moïse smiled.

"They're my partners."

"Partners?" I said, frowning.

"Sure," replied Moïse, nodding. "We delivered supplies to the gold miners, back in Nez Perce County."

"Mules?"

"Yes," said Moïse. "They're smart animals. And they have better stamina, and can carry heavier loads, than a horse. There were no roads to the mines, so the conditions were tough and the mules are naturally cautious."

Moïse pointed to the mule with the light-coloured coat.

"She's my bell mare."

"What's a bell mare?"

"She's the top mule. The one all the others would follow," he explained. "When we camped out, and had to round them up at daybreak, one of the packers would go out into the hills to find her, ring the bell that she wore around her neck, and the other mules would start moving toward her and follow her into camp."

"Almost like the lead ox."

Moïse nodded, and I smiled.

"How many mules did you have?"

"Sometimes up to one hundred in a train," he replied. "Each mule had a packsaddle loaded with supplies and wore a bridle. All of the bridles were secured together, and the mules would walk in single file. We'd head for the mining camps. The miners would arrive back at the camps on Sundays. Once they were there, we'd unpack and sell the goods that we'd carried in."

"You'd sell them goods?"

"Yes," Moïse nodded. "I owned the cargo."

"And you'd use these mules?"

"Yes, some of them. I got rid of a few. Some were just down-right mean." Moïse laughed. "They'd rub their packs off against a tree or would lie down and try to roll them loose."

"Why'd you stop doing this work?"

"After I bought the land here in the valley," he replied, "I continued packing supplies up Catherine Creek to the mines around Auburn in Baker County. But it's a tough business, and I needed a break. I opened the mill and began raising horses."

Moïse taught me how to run the farm. Although there were farm-hands that helped out, there was a herd of dairy cows to milk each day and a large vegetable garden to weed, in addition to the large herd of racing horses that required attention. With so many horses, there were cuts and scrapes that needed tending to, particularly with the young horses that bucked and played and bickered with each other for hours on end, every day. I began to care for the horses.

"Whoa, pretty girl," I said soothingly to a young sorrel-coloured horse named Poppy.

Her coat was almost the colour of buckskin, and her mane and tail were orange, peppered with black and white hairs. She had a dark strip down the top of her back and dark stripes at the tops of her legs. And there was a beautiful cloud-shaped patch of white hair on one side of her rump, as if someone had dropped a sack of flour on her.

"What did she do?" Moïse asked, as he approached.

"She has a cut on her side," I explained. "I'm going to clean it."

"I'll help," said Moïse.

He grabbed the rope attached to her halter. Poppy became nervous and began to pull backward.

"Whoa," Moïse told her, but she kept pulling.

I took the rope from him, and Poppy stopped pulling and calmed down.

"That's a girl," I told her softly, while I cleaned out the cut on her side.

"She likes women," said Moïse

I nodded, feeling proud.

"She's a beauty."

"Would you like to ride her?" he asked.

I stared for a moment, and then nodded again and smiled.

Moïse found a bridle and a saddle to fit Poppy, and began helping me train her. Although she was saddle-broke, she was still very green. Poppy had a sweet disposition though, and was constantly listening for my voice commands. She felt different from Grace, bigger but more finely built and with a very soft mouth.

I began riding almost daily. Most days I'd ride Poppy, but sometimes, when I wanted to go for a long quiet walk, I'd hop onto Grace bareback and we'd ride along the valley. I was content and couldn't believe my good fortune. I had two horses that I could take out for a ride whenever I wished.

"Not riding again today?" Moïse asked me one day later that fall, when the leaves were changing colours in the valley, although the sun still felt warm.

"I'm feeling a bit queasy these days," I replied.

I'd begun to feel a bit off, particularly when I rode.

"We'll get you in to see Dr. Renaud," Moïse suggested, looking concerned.

"No," I said, as I shook my head. "It's nothing. I'm sure I'll be fine."

I disliked visiting the doctor. I felt quite competent in my own abilities to heal people and didn't feel the need to see someone else.

"How long have you felt unwell?" he asked.

I shrugged.

"Just a couple of weeks."

"That's too long, Julia."

"I'm fine," I told him. "I still have an appetite, and energy, and am not coughing or sick. It'll pass."

Moïse stared pointedly.

"Okay," I told him. "I'll talk to Martha."

The next day, I went to visit Martha at her house.

"How are you, Julia?" Martha asked, preparing tea and biscuits for us.

"I'm fine," I replied. "Although I've felt a bit queasy lately. Moïse's concerned."

Martha smiled at me and took my hands. "You're pregnant."

"Pregnant?" This was something that hadn't occurred to me. I shook my head. "No, I don't think so."

She nodded and smiled, and then squeezed my hands. "I'm sure of it. Let's get you an appointment with Dr. Renaud to confirm."

A visit to Dr. Renaud confirmed Martha's prediction. I was pregnant. Moïse was elated with the news and caught me up in a hug.

"No more riding horses for you!" he told me, putting me back down on my feet and leading me to a chair.

"What! Why?"

I stared at him. I felt that I was getting somewhere with Poppy. I didn't want to stop working with her now.

Moïse was adamant.

"It's too dangerous."

I scowled.

The next day, Moïse returned home with a black, shiny buggy. It had large wheels and was built for two people.

"What's this for?" I asked, as he led me outside to see it.

"It's for you." Moïse told me, proudly.

I shook my head.

"I can't drive a buggy."

"I'll teach you," he replied. "And, we'll train Poppy to pull it."

"Poppy could pull this?"

He nodded.

I liked this idea. I could continue working with her and would have the freedom to come and go as I pleased.

The first day that Moïse harnessed Poppy up to the buggy, she stood quietly. And when she began pulling it, she didn't balk at the sound of the wagon behind her or at the sound of the wheels crunching over the gravel below. She looked very elegant harnessed to the buggy and seemed to lift her knees higher as she trotted along.

Before the year was out, my first child was born. We named him Edouard, after Moïse's brother.

Edouard was a good baby. He was always happy, and although I was tired from the lack of sleep, I had plenty of help from Victoria, Martha, and the other neighbours.

"I'll take Edouard for a walk," Victoria said one night, after supper.

"Oh, he'd love that," I said, giving Victoria's shoulder a squeeze.

I was worried about her. She'd always been a slight girl, and although she was now twelve years old, she was often taken for someone much younger. As a result, I tended to coddle her more than I should have done. Lately, I'd noticed the melancholy expression she always wore. I knew she was pleased that she'd moved with me to Oregon, but I also knew that she desperately missed Joseph, Kimi, and Koko. And she missed living on the wide-open prairie, where we'd pick up camp and moved to a new location regularly.

My heart ached for her as I watched her carry Edouard outside, her face becoming animated as she spoke to him. I walked back to the kitchen table and began to clean up the supper dishes.

"Should I send her back to Koko?" I asked Moïse.

He looked up from the newspaper that he was reading and frowned.

"Victoria?"

I nodded. "I'm worried about her."

He shook his head. "She has more opportunities here."

"Yes," I agreed, "but it's been such a change for her."

"Wait until she makes more friends," he replied. "It'll make a difference."

I encouraged Victoria to spend more time with Amelie and some of the other French Canadian girls close to her age. At first, she did, but one day she stopped going out.

"What happened?" I asked one afternoon, as Victoria moped about the house.

She shrugged.

"Did something happen?"

Victoria looked at me with tears in her eyes. "I want to go back," she whispered.

"Back?" I asked, as I stared at her face.

She nodded. "With Koko."

A lump formed in my throat. "Why?" I asked.

"I can't speak French," she cried.

"But you're relearning it. You've picked it up quickly."

"I have an accent," she cried. "And they think that I'm stupid."

I stared at her. "Stupid?"

She nodded.

"You're anything but stupid, Victoria," I said, rubbing my hand up and down her arm.

"But I've never been to school," she said, with tears in her eyes.

"Neither have I."

"But you remember how to speak French. I don't."

She pursed her lips. "And I can't read or write either. All the other girls can."

"We never had a chance to learn," I replied, sadly.

Papa had started teaching me, but we never got very far. And we never had the opportunity when we lived with Koko.

I looked at Victoria and smiled. "But Moïse can."

Again, she shrugged.

"I'll get him to teach you!"

Victoria smiled, but seemed unconvinced.

Moïse began to teach Victoria how to read. She caught on quickly and studied fastidiously, practicing at every opportunity. Moïse was wonderful, purchasing books for her, and she became an avid reader. She'd sit with Edouard and read stories to him. Edouard would stare at the pictures in the books and ask Victoria to read and reread the stories to him. I'd listen to them as I prepared supper. I fondly remembered when Papa used to read the Bible to us at the kitchen table, while Mama cleaned up after a meal. I loved those times.

Often, mealtimes would include one or more of Moïse's bachelor friends. I didn't mind the extra company. I'd developed a love for cooking and found this a good opportunity to practice my skills and try out a new dish that Martha, or one of the other women, gave me to try. And invariably, the conversations would revolve around horses.

"Did you see LeBoeuf's new stallion?" a neighbour named Gerry asked Moïse one evening after supper. "He's a beauty!"

He whistled.

"I saw him exercising yesterday," Moïse nodded. "He'll be tough to beat. But I wonder if he'll be good at the longer distances?"

"I thought the same," Gerry agreed. "He's stocky and not too tall."

Moïse nodded. "Yes, he's very powerful."

I was captivated by the conversation. Everyone in the valley raised racehorses, and the conversations always seemed to migrate to bloodlines, or training methods, or racing.

"Why does that matter?" I asked.

Moïse smiled at me.

"He's powerful, but might not have the ability to last at a longer distance. He looks like he'd be better at the shorter races."

I soaked up this tidbit of information and examined the horses in the fields to figure out for myself what they were referring to. On some weekends, Moïse or another neighbour hosted a race. The neighbours would bring their mounts, and the horses were raced around galloping paths built around the outsides of the horse pastures. There wasn't a prize at stake for these races. Rather, and probably more importantly, they raced for bragging rights.

One evening when Edouard was almost two, and I was heavily pregnant with my second child, I heard the familiar sound of Moïse's wagon on the driveway. Having learned the routine from Victoria, Edouard raced to the window and began waving and smiling broadly.

"Papa! Papa!" he cried, happily.

"Is Papa home?" I asked, smiling.

"Papa! Papa!" Edouard repeated, clapping his hands and dancing and running about the kitchen.

"Did he bring company?" I asked Victoria, who was setting the table.

She walked to the window and pushed back the lace curtain.

"There's a man with him."

"Do you recognize him?" I asked.

She shrugged her shoulders and shook her head. "He looks older and has grey hair."

I frowned. Not many of Moïse's friends had gray hair.

"Set an extra place, please," I asked, turning back to the mashed potatoes that I was spooning into a serving bowl.

"Hello!" Moïse called out, as he walked in through the door.

"Papa!" Edouard squealed, leaping into Moïse's arms.

"Hello!"

Moïse kissed his son's head and placed him on the floor. Then he took off his hat and hung it on a hook by the door, before removing his jacket and placing it on the adjacent wooden peg. He walked over to me and softly kissed my cheek.

"How are you, Julia?"

"Fine," I replied, with a smile. "Wash up. Supper's nearly ready."

He didn't move and continued to smile broadly at me.

"What?" I asked, looking from him to the door and back. "Where's your guest?"

Moïse looked as if he could hardly contain his excitement.

"What is it, Moïse?"

"Come with me," he said, taking hold of my arm. "I have a surprise for you."

"Wait, wait."

I put down the spoon and rubbed my hands on the tea towel.

Moïse grabbed my hand.

"I was at the sawmill today," he said, pulling me toward the door. "And a man walked in. They were especially busy."

That didn't surprise me. The recent movement of people into the area, and the building that accompanied it, meant that the sawmill was in high demand.

"I began talking to him and found out that he was also French Canadian."

I thought nothing of this, since all of Moïse's friends were French Canadian.

"He moved from Canada in the 1830s and worked as a fur trapper and trader," he continued.

This brought back memories of my childhood. I felt a lump form in my throat and tried to blink back tears. Moïse put his arm around me.

"Then he settled on a farm in Iowa," he added, pausing as he stared at me. "And I think that he's someone you'll want to meet."

He opened the door.

CHAPTER 11

I caught my breath and felt as if I was going to faint. Moïse put his arm around me and led me to a seat on the porch. I sat down, then looked at the man. He stood at the bottom of the porch steps and held the brim of his hat in front of his chest with both hands. He was blinking back tears.

"Papa?" I whispered.

He nodded and pursed his lips. I saw the bump in his throat move up and down as he swallowed.

"Oh, Papa," I whispered, closing my eyes. "I thought that you were dead."

Moïse put his arm around me, and I sobbed onto his shoulder.

"I didn't see you. I only saw Mama falling to the ground."

There was the sound of little footsteps on the porch, and I looked up.

"And who are you?" Papa asked, bending down.

"Edouard."

"I'm pleased to meet you, Edouard," said Papa, extending his hand. "My name's Peter."

I smiled. Victoria stood near the door, looking from me to Papa. I stood up and walked over to her.

"It's Papa," I told her quietly, wiping my tears with my sleeve.

She nodded, and stared at Papa. I held her hand, and we walked over to him. Tears were streaming down Papa's face, and I stepped forward to hug him. I inhaled deeply. He smelled like the Papa that I remembered: a mix of fresh air and soap. I stood back and studied his face. His deep-set blue eyes were still intense, but had faded slightly, and were now framed by bushy grey eyebrows. His thick dark hair was now thin, and mostly silver.

I turned to Victoria. "Do you remember Papa?"

She had tears in her eyes. She shook her head, and then ran into the house.

I squeezed my eyes shut and blinked quickly, trying to push back the tears. I reached out and took Papa's hand.

"Come inside," I smiled. "Supper's ready."

The meal was awkward. We tried to keep the conversation light, talking about the farm, the racehorses, and Moïse's mill. Papa told us that he'd recently purchased land nearby in the valley. I covered my mouth. This was his dream, his second chance, and the reason for us heading west all those years ago.

After supper, once the table was cleared and the supper dishes washed, Moïse took Edouard outside for a walk by the horses. Papa, Victoria, and I sat down at the table to talk.

"Where's Mama?" I finally asked.

"She's dead," he answered, quietly.

I covered my mouth with my hand, and then busied myself serving tea. Deep down, I always suspected this, but it was still a shock to have it confirmed.

"What happened that night?" I finally asked as I set down the teapot. "I saw Mama and . . ." My voice cracked.

"I saw Victoria and Joseph being taken," I continued. "But I couldn't see you. I called your name, Papa, but you didn't answer."

"They spooked the oxen, and they bolted away," replied Papa, a pained expression on his face. "I chased after them. I had to.

Without them, we had no means to travel. But when I got back many hours later, your mother was dead, and I couldn't find you." He swallowed hard.

"She was dead?" Sobs began to wrack my body. "I never knew. I hoped that she'd just been hurt and would search for us."

Papa nodded.

"Did you bury Mama?" I asked, through my tears.

"Yes," he whispered. "I buried her nearby, and then searched and searched for you, but there was no sign of you anywhere. Then I hitched up the wagon, and travelled back to Fort Laramie for help."

He stopped speaking abruptly and knitted his thick brows together.

"But I met up with members of the posse that had been searching for me."

His voice broke, and he took a drink of his tea before continuing.

"They turned me in." He spat out the words and knitted his brows again. "I had to spend time in jail for the murder, instead of searching for you!"

He paused for a moment before composing himself.

"When they finally released me," he continued, "I went back to see the older boys."

"And how are they?" I asked.

"They're well," he smiled, sadly. "Grandmother took care of them."

I smiled at the mention of her.

"Alex is married and has a family. Same with Harold. And the two younger boys are working."

"But how did you know to look here?" I asked, frowning.

"I didn't," he replied, smiling. "Your grandmother's dying wish was for me to find you," he replied, his voice cracking now.

"She's dead?" I asked, tears filling my eyes.

He nodded.

"She told me to find you, Julia. She loved you."

I nodded, as the tears spilled onto my cheeks.

"I didn't know where to go, so I headed west again. I spoke to people on the way, but no one had news about you. Then I finally decided that I needed to purchase some land and found a small farm close to here on the same side of the valley." He smiled. "And like everyone else, I needed wood to build a house and met Moïse at the sawmill."

I stood up and walked over to hug him, and then sat back down. Victoria sat still and didn't say a word.

"What happened with you?" Papa asked, and then whispered. "Where's Joseph?"

"He's grown into a fine boy," I replied, smiling. "He reminds me of you."

"What happened?" he asked.

"We were captured."

He frowned.

"By who?"

"The Blackfoot."

Papa hit his hand on the table.

"They killed your mother and then kidnapped you!"

He scowled, and that familiar expression appeared on his face—the one that used to appear before he lost his temper.

I nodded and glanced at Victoria. Her eyes were wide, and she looked scared. I put my hand reassuringly over hers.

"And Joseph's with them now? How could you leave him there?" he said angrily as he stood up, knocking his chair backward. "I'm going after him."

"Papa," I told him. "Sit down. Please."

At first, he looked angrily at me, and then seemed to remember that I was no longer a child. I waited for him to sit before continuing.

"Yes, Joseph is still there. We were adopted by a wonderful woman named Koko. She's the sister of the chief, and her husband had been killed some time before we met her. And she has two children the same age as Victoria and Joseph."

I looked at Victoria. She was wiping away tears.

"Koko took good care of us. She loved us as her own."

Papa stared at me. I could see different expressions cross his face: hatred, relief, bewilderment, sadness, and back to hatred.

"How can that be?" he spat. "They killed your mother. And kidnapped you!"

"Papa, please," I continued. "I resented them at first. I resented her for the longest time. I didn't want a new mother. I didn't want a new family, particularly after what they did to ours. But we needed someone to care for us. I was just a child, and Victoria and Joseph were so young. She was there for us when we had no one else—when I needed help."

Papa began sobbing quietly. He took out a handkerchief and blew his nose loudly.

"Victoria and Joseph don't remember any other family. And when I married Moïse, they were given the choice to stay or come with me. This was a very tough decision for both of them."

I paused, with tears filling my eyes.

"And for me."

Victoria began to sob. I hugged her hard against me.

"I'm not sure that we made the correct decision for Victoria. She misses Koko and Kimi terribly, along with the freedom of the life that she lived there. But there are more opportunities here for her."

Papa nodded.

"It's also been difficult moving away from the Blackfoot," I added, smiling softly. "They were the first people, and maybe the only people, to fully accept us as their own."

CHAPTER 12

Papa settled into his new life in Union County and soon became involved in the construction that was taking place all over the surrounding area. Back in Iowa, he and Uncle Henri had built a bridge over the Nishnabotna River. Papa had spent an entire summer travelling the length of the river, scouting potential building sites for the crossing, before finally deciding on an outcrop of bedrock as the ideal building site for the bridge. They'd felled trees in the heavily wooded land nearby and floated the large pine timbers down the river, stockpiling them on the shore, waiting for winter and the cold to set in.

As a child, I'd visited the bridge in the dead of winter, when the river was frozen solid and the construction was at full tilt. They'd craft heavy stringers into diamond-shaped cribs on the ice's surface and fill the cribs with rocks. In the springtime, once the river thawed, the weighted cribs would settle onto the bottom of the streambed and the upper structure of the bridge would be built on top of them.

Now, many years later, Papa was building a bridge over a creek that flowed down from the Blue Mountains through his land and toward the Grande River. A toll road that he was building across his property would cross the creek at this location.

"You should be at home, child," Papa scolded Edouard softly, before lifting him into the air and twirling him around.

Edouard giggled, throwing back his head and opening his mouth, trying to catch a big fluffy snowflake on his tongue. He'd accompanied me on the sleigh ride to deliver Papa his lunch. There was a fresh blanket of snow, and Edouard had giggled and clapped as we'd driven the sleigh through it.

Papa lowered Edouard to the ground and tightened the scarf around his face, then turned to me. I handed him a pail filled with his lunch.

"Thank you," he replied, smiling.

"How's the bridge work?" I asked, turning and walking back toward Poppy and the sleigh that I'd stopped near his house.

"Very good! The creek froze solid, and so early!" Papa replied, clapping his mitten-covered hands. "We're ahead of schedule."

He looked around and frowned.

"Where's the baby?"

"Victoria's watching her," I said, climbing back into the sleigh.

My daughter Philomène had been born at the end of the summer.

"We have to get back."

Once I was in the sleigh, Papa lifted Edouard and settled him beside me. I covered our laps with a rug, and clucked at Poppy. She began trotting, the strap of bells around her neck jingling as she pranced.

"Thanks for lunch," Papa called after us.

I lifted my hand in acknowledgement.

Later that afternoon, a horse-drawn sleigh raced up to the house, before the kitchen door was flung open.

"Julia!" Papa shouted.

I ran toward the door.

"He's been hurt!"

Papa had his arm under a man's shoulders, supporting him as he walked. There was blood seeping from the man's outer thigh.

"Bring him through here," I said, hurrying towards the spare bedroom down the hallway from the kitchen. "Put him onto the bed."

The man cried out in pain as Papa lowered him onto the bed.

"Who is he?" I asked, removing one of the man's knee-length boots.

"His name's François," Papa replied as he slipped off the man's other boot. "He works for me."

I peered at the wound on the man's leg. The worst of the bleeding appeared to have stopped.

"What happened?" I asked.

"We were loading the sleigh, and the mules spooked," Papa explained. "François jumped onto the sleigh, and grabbed hold of the reins. The mules were galloping, but he got them under control and managed to slow them down. But then the runner of the sleigh hit something hard under the snow, probably a frozen rut. The sleigh rocked, bouncing François over the front of it, between the sleigh and the mules."

I caught my breath.

"Somehow, he managed to grab hold of the front of the sleigh," Papa continued. "He was pulling himself back up onto it when one of the mules kicked out and got him on his leg. The impact threw him off the sleigh and thankfully out of the way of the runners."

I winced, and looked back at François. He was pale and beginning to shake.

"Take off his jacket," I told Papa. "And grab some more firewood. We need to heat up this room."

"Victoria," I called down the hallway. "Grab some more blankets."

I ran for my medicine bag. I no longer used the pouch that Grandmother had given to me many years before. Now that I tended to the cuts on the horses, I'd graduated to a bigger buckskin bag, in which I could store larger quantities of plants. I'd adorned the bag with a quillwork design using quills that I'd dyed black, red, and yellow, just as Grandmother had shown me.

In the kitchen, I boiled strawberry roots, created a poultice of purple coneflower roots, and then returned to the bedroom. In the hearth, Papa had built a roaring fire that was giving off a great deal of heat, and the room felt much warmer. Victoria had covered François with additional blankets. He was no longer shaking and seemed to have a little more colour.

I knelt near the side of the bed and cut away the material surrounding the wound on the side of François' leg. The cut wasn't long but looked deep. From its shape, it looked as though the tip of the mule's toe had pierced the skin. The area surrounding the cut was beginning to swell, although there was no bruising. I gingerly felt the bones surrounding the cut. François cried out in pain and sat up.

"Sorry," I murmured.

Papa and Victoria grabbed hold of his shoulders and gently lay him back against the bed.

"Is it broken?" François asked, hoarsely.

I shook my head.

"No, you were very lucky. But there's a lot of swelling, as well as a cut."

I cleaned out the wound with the liquid from the boiled strawberries, and applied the coneflower poultice. I then stood up and looked at François. His eyes were closed, and he seemed to be resting more comfortably.

François stayed with us during his convalescence. The wound healed without infection and the swelling was kept at bay with the application of the coneflower compresses.

"There it is," I told Victoria as I removed the compress on the fifth day.

"It's blue and purple," she said, wrinkling her nose.

"Yes," I replied. "The bruising was deep and has only just now come to the surface."

I turned to François.

"You're very lucky that you didn't break your bone."

"His foot musta glanced off my leg," François replied, smiling from me to Victoria. "It was your Pa's ornery mule that got me."

Victoria frowned slightly and turned away, and then hurried out of the room.

By the end of the week, François was back on his feet working with Papa, although still walking with a limp. François became a regular suppertime guest at our house. Although he was also from Québec, François wasn't a childhood friend of Moïse's. The two had met some years earlier when they'd worked together felling trees.

About a month later, Papa and François joined us for supper.

"Grand-Papa!" Edouard shouted, running to the door.

Papa caught him in his arms and twirled him around.

"Hello, François," said Moïse. "Come in. Let me take your coat."

Moïse hung up François' coat, then led him into the house.

"Hello, François," I called out from the counter, where I stood slicing a ham.

"Hello, Julia," he replied, warmly.

"Victoria," Moïse called.

She'd suddenly disappeared into her bedroom at the sound of François' voice.

"Your papa and François are here."

There was silence for a moment, then Victoria walked back into the kitchen and resumed setting the kitchen table.

"Hello, Victoria," François greeted her, smiling.

Victoria stopped. Her eyes darted up at him, and she murmured a quick hello before turning away. I carried the serving plate of ham to the table, and put my arm around her shoulder and squeezed.

"It's okay," I whispered.

Over supper, François peppered Victoria with questions, trying to draw her into the conversation. But whenever she could, Victoria would only give a one-word answer, causing the thread of conversation to die and forcing François to pick up another one. He wasn't deterred.

"Have you heard of the Kentucky Derby?" he asked Victoria.

She frowned and shook her head.

"It's a horse race," he explained. "The first race was held last year."

"A horse race?" asked Moïse. "Where at?"

"Churchill Downs, in Louisville, Kentucky," François replied. "The winner took home almost $3,000!"

Moïse whistled, but Victoria looked disinterested.

"And two years before that," François continued, "there was a big race in Baltimore called the Preakness, and the purse was over $2,000!"

He turned to Victoria.

"Where'd you grow up?"

She stopped eating and stared at him. Tears filled her eyes, she asked to be excused, and fled from the table down the hallway to her bedroom.

"Pardon me," François murmured, looking puzzled. "I didn't mean anything by this question."

Papa shook his head and knitted his thick brows.

"She had a traumatic childhood."

"No, Papa," I said, adamantly. "Her childhood was far from traumatic."

He frowned at me and shook his head again, and then looked away.

I looked at François and smiled. "She had a wonderful childhood."

François looked confused. I explained to him how our family had been ambushed while travelling west and how Victoria, Joseph, and I had been captured by the Blackfoot and raised as their own. I looked up at Papa. It frustrated me that anytime Joseph's name was mentioned, Papa's temper would flare.

"Where's Joseph now?" François asked. "I don't think that I've met him."

"He still lives with Koko, our adopted mother," I explained.

"He's still with the Blackfoot?" asked François.

I nodded.

"He was just a baby when we were adopted by her. She's like his mother."

Papa slammed his hand against the table. "She's not his mother!"

François looked from Papa to me.

"When I married Moïse," I explained, "Joseph was given the choice to stay with Koko and the Blackfoot or to come with Moïse and me. Victoria was also given this choice." I paused before continuing. "It was a tough decision."

"And Joseph chose to stay?" asked François.

I nodded. "He has a good life there. Koko loves him, as does Machk, her son. Machk and Joseph are very close in age. They're like brothers."

"He has brothers of his own!" Papa retorted.

"Papa," I said calmly, staring at him. "I know that. And Joseph knows that. But he was just a baby when he last saw them, and he doesn't remember his brothers."

Papa stood up from the table and walked to the window.

"And Victoria's torn," said François, quietly, "between her life with the Blackfoot and this one."

I smiled. "She's still trying to find her place. She's even had to relearn French."

This didn't deter François. If anything, he became even more determined to befriend Victoria after that night. After supper, he'd ask her to accompany him on a walk, or would ask her to a dance held at one of the neighbours' properties. Soon, we began to hear Victoria laugh again. Before the year was out, François asked Victoria to marry him.

CHAPTER 13

"Victoria," I called over my shoulder.

She didn't reply.

"Victoria," I called again.

I glanced at the clock that sat on the chest of drawers at the end of the bed. It was after ten thirty, and she was due to be married at eleven o'clock.

"We have to leave."

Still there was no answer. I took one last look at my reflection in the mirror and patted my hair, which was pulled up and secured on the top of my head. The ends of my hair had been curled and cascaded down the back of my neck. Just as she'd done on my wedding day, Martha had created an elaborate hairstyle for Victoria, and also for me. She'd taken Edouard and Philomène home with her to care for them during the ceremony, so that I could tend to Victoria.

The heels of my slipper-covered feet clicked on the wooden floor, as I walked down the hallway to Victoria's room. They were the prettiest shoes that I'd ever owned and looked elegant on my feet, although my toes were beginning to feel cold and numb. They weren't accustomed to being wedged into this type of rigid V-shaped structure.

I found Victoria staring at her reflection in the mirror that stood on her bureau. Her face was pale, and her eyes looked scared.

"There you are," I said cheerfully, walking over to her and squeezing her shoulders.

She turned and threw her arms about me. I hugged her, blinking back tears that suddenly welled in my eyes.

"I can't go through with this," she whispered.

"Shh," I said, softly. "Now, stop crying. Your eyes will be red and puffy."

I handed her a soft handkerchief, and led her to the edge of the bed, where she sat down.

"François is a good man. He's kind and hard-working," I said, smiling. "You'll have a good life with him."

"Yes," she said, nodding, but then frowned. "But I just don't know if I want this."

"This?"

"This life. Some days, I feel like I can't breathe."

"You never really knew this world. We were already on the run by the time you were born."

"Some days," she said, staring out the window, "I long to put my feet in a creek, or watch the sun set on the horizon, or listen to the coyotes in the distance on a cold winter night when the fire casts a warm glow in the tipi."

She turned to me and smiled sadly.

"And Koko?" I whispered.

She nodded.

"I miss her. I know that Papa doesn't like to hear about her. But Julia," she said, looking at me with tears in her eyes, "she was my mother. And she loved me."

"She still does," I said, smiling softly. "Would you like to go back?"

She shrugged.

There was a knock on the bedroom doorframe. I turned around and saw Papa standing at the door. He had tears in his eyes.

"May I come in?" he asked.

I nodded.

He walked to the middle of the bedroom and stopped in front of Victoria.

"I came to get you for the ceremony and overheard part of your conversation. I apologize for this."

He cleared his throat.

"I know that you don't feel a connection with me, and this saddens me like you can't imagine."

He drew a handkerchief out of his pocket and blew his nose.

"But I love you, Victoria. I always have."

She pursed her lips. Papa took hold of her hand lightly.

"I know that I've been critical about your life with the Blackfoot, and of your adoptive mother."

Victoria frowned and shook her head slightly.

"Her name's Koko."

"Your life with Koko," he said softly, bowing his head slightly. "I've been unkind, and this has hurt you. But I've found it difficult to hear about your happy memories with them."

Papa's voice cracked. He cleared his throat and continued.

"I'm torn. I'm grateful that they took such good care of you and made you happy. But I'm also angry that they stole you from me. I should have lived these moments with you. They should be part of my memories too."

Papa swallowed hard and seemed to be having difficulty catching his breath. I pushed a wooden chair toward him. He sat down and then continued.

"I now realize that I was wrong, and I promise that I'll stop making you feel guilty for these memories, or for your feelings for

Koko," he said, smiling sadly. He paused, and then continued. "Or for leaving Joseph behind."

Tears streamed down Papa's face. "Please, forgive me."

"Oh, Papa," Victoria whispered, throwing her arms around his neck.

Papa held Victoria tightly, and then held her away from him at arm's length.

"Now, don't we have a wedding to attend?" he asked her, softly.

Victoria looked from him to me, and smiled.

At precisely eleven o'clock, the music of the Wedding March began. Remi and Gerry played it on a fiddle and the piano that Moïse had moved from the house into the new barn, which had been raised in time for the October wedding. The guests were seated in chairs that faced an altar, built for the couple and the priest to stand on while the vows were exchanged. There was an aisle down the centre of the barn, splitting the rows of chairs in half and defined by wreaths of flowers and white ribbons that were stretched out along down the aisle's length. The doors to the new barn were thrown open, allowing the morning sunlight to fill its interior. The sunlight cast a beautiful glow on the yellow and orange flowers that decorated the windows, adorned the walls, and covered the posts and beams of the vaulted ceiling. A sweet perfume wafted from the flowers and mingled with the fresh wood smell of the new barn's interior.

François and his best man, Moïse, led the way down the aisle, followed by Father Jean, the priest. Once the men neared the altar, François stepped up onto it and turned to face the barn doors, as Papa and Victoria slowly progressed down the aisle. Papa held Victoria's hand tightly in the bend of his arm and beamed proudly. When they reached the altar, François extended his arm, bowed his head slightly, and shook Papa's hand. Papa gave Victoria a kiss on her cheek and gave her hand to François.

Victoria looked beautiful. She wore a lavender silk dress, with a tight-fitting bodice and high neckline, and full-length fitted sleeves. The skirt was elaborately draped, and puffed with an abundance of material that was trimmed with delicate lace and orange blossoms resembling swan's down. Although I wasn't the mother of the bride, Victoria had insisted that I wear a dress of richly embroidered black silk and stand next to Papa during the ceremony.

"Go in peace," Father Jean told the couple at the end of the proceedings, before Victoria and François turned to face their guests for the first time as a married couple.

Victoria and François moved into a house that Papa, Moïse, and François had built on a piece of land adjoining ours. I continued to visit with Victoria daily, driving the buggy the short distance down the valley to her new farm. Edouard and Philomène enjoyed these trips. They loved to see Victoria and really enjoyed travelling in the buggy.

One warm afternoon several months after the wedding, Victoria prepared a picnic lunch. We all sat at a large blanket that she'd spread out for us below a small grove of trees near her house. Once we'd finished eating the goodies that she'd packed in a large wicker basket, and the children were running through the grass barefoot, she'd told me the news.

"I'm pregnant!" she'd exclaimed.

Later that day, when we'd returned home, I applied the break on the buggy and climbed down, smiling. Victoria seemed happy. Edouard and Philomène had fallen asleep on the trip home following the picnic. I picked Philomène up into my arms and took hold of Edouard's hand, and then started towards the house. I noticed two unfamiliar horses grazing between the house and the barn and stopped to look at them for a moment. I frowned. These weren't our horses, but fearing that I couldn't hold Philomène in my arms for much longer, I turned and hurried to the house.

As we neared the porch, I noticed a man sitting in the chair outside the parlour window and another lounging against the railing of the porch. Both men stood up as we approached. I froze.

CHAPTER 14

"Julia!" one of the men called to me.

I shrieked. "Joseph? Machk?"

Philomène woke in my arms and began crying, while Edouard grabbed hold of my leg.

"It's okay," I told them.

"I'll put them down for their naps," I told Joseph in Blackfoot, and hurried into the house.

When I returned to the porch, Joseph rose again from his seat.

"Oh, Joseph!" I cried.

I grabbed him, pulling him into a big hug, and then held him away from me. He was taller than me now and had filled out. I grabbed Machk into a hug too.

"Machk!" I cried, holding him close. "Look at how you've grown! Sit, please!"

I took a seat on one of the chairs.

"What are you two doing here?"

"I wanted to see you," Joseph replied quietly.

"I've thought of you every day," I said, smiling.

"Where's Victoria?" asked Joseph.

"We just came from her house. We had lunch with her. She was married last fall, and she just told us that she's pregnant!"

Joseph and Machk smiled.

"How's Koko?" I asked.

"She's doing well," Machk replied. "She was really sad after you and Victoria left, but we kept her busy!"

He laughed.

"She sends her love, Julia," Joseph added. "And she's anxious to hear any news about you and Victoria."

I smiled and tears filled my eyes.

"And Kimi?"

"She was just married in the spring," said Joseph.

"Married," I said, smiling. "Oh, Victoria will be so happy to hear this news. Did you just get here?"

Joseph nodded.

"I'm sorry. I'm forgetting my manners," I said, standing up. "You're probably thirsty after your trip. I'll grab you something to drink."

I ran into the house, the screen door slamming shut behind me. In the kitchen, I poured some water from the cheesecloth-covered pitcher and arranged some cookies onto a plate. I heard a wagon drive down the road and stop outside the barn. It seemed to be a little early for Moïse to be home, but I thought nothing of it. He often put in long days at the mill and sometimes surprised us by taking an afternoon off to spend with family.

I placed the glasses and plate of cookies onto a tray and carried it toward the door. I was just in time to hear Papa growling.

"Get away from the house!"

I stopped in my tracks. What was he doing? Then it dawned on me. I set the tray down on a table and ran out the screen door.

"No, Papa!" I exclaimed.

"Julia!" he shouted, as he pointed a gun at Joseph and Machk. "Go back into the house! I'll get rid of these Indians!"

"No, Papa!" I cried. "It's Joseph!"

Papa froze.

"Put the gun down," I told him.

Papa lowered the gun and sank to his knees.

"It's Papa," I told Joseph and Machk in Blackfoot. "He was just protecting us."

I ran down the steps to Papa and helped him back to his feet. I led him up the steps and sat him on the chair that Joseph had vacated.

"Put the gun away, Papa," I said.

Papa did as I asked, and stared at Joseph.

"What are you doing here?" he asked Joseph in French.

Joseph simply stared and shook his head, and looked at me.

"Papa," I replied, quietly. "Joseph doesn't speak French."

"Doesn't speak French!" Papa's voice boomed, before he scowled at me. "Why didn't you teach him?"

Joseph and Machk walked down the few steps and stood on the ground in front of the porch.

"Papa!" I said, frowning at him. "I was just a child myself."

"How did you find him?" Joseph asked me quietly, looking nervously at Papa.

"I didn't."

I quickly explained to Joseph and Machk how Papa had found us.

"Why's he here?" Papa asked me, staring at Joseph.

"He wanted to see Victoria and me."

"He looks like one of them!" Papa hushed at me, scowling.

I smiled from Papa to Joseph.

"I think that he looks wonderful."

Joseph and Machk joined us for supper. I had Papa ride over to Victoria's and invite them for supper. Victoria's eyes sparkled, as she and the two boys swapped stories of our childhood.

"Remember when we got stung by wasps?" Machk asked, his eyes twinkling.

"Yes, I do," I replied. "That was my first chance to heal someone on my own."

"And how Machk told you and Koko that we'd stepped on the nest?" said Joseph laughing. "We were throwing sticks and rocks at it!"

Both boys began laughing.

"And I actually felt sorry for you!" I said, with a chuckle. "And what happened to your pony?"

"I still have him," replied Joseph, proudly. "He's old now."

"I was so jealous of you," I said.

"You tried to take him from me!"

Moïse smiled at me.

"She's still mad about horses."

Although his Blackfoot was limited and rusty, he still was able to follow our conversation.

"Do you still have Grace?" Joseph asked.

I nodded and smiled.

"Would you like to see her?"

"Why don't you take Joseph to see Grace?" Moïse suggested. "I'll take care of things here."

I led Joseph towards the horses' fields. We walked slowly, and I could tell that something was troubling him. I linked my arm through his.

"Everything okay?" I asked.

He nudged me gently with his shoulder as we walked and smiled.

"You could always read me. I missed you so much after you left."

I could see tears in his eyes and nodded.

"I felt the same about you."

"Koko's so wonderful," he continued. "And I'm happy. But at the same time, I feel a longing for something."

I nodded. "You feel torn?"

"Yes," he said. "I didn't notice until you left."

"Have you spoken to Koko about this?"

"This is partly why I'm here. She suggested that I visit you."

I smiled and tears filled my eyes. That sounded so like Koko.

"I miss her so much," I whispered.

He smiled. "She told me to talk to you."

"I like my life here," I said, and then pointed to the little black horse that was grazing a short distance away. "There she is."

At the sound of my voice, Grace lifted her head and whinnied to me, then began sauntering toward us.

"She looks great!" said Joseph. "And she's hardly limping."

"Her leg healed nicely. Papa's begun teaching Edouard to ride her. She's so patient and kind."

"Just like you then!"

I turned and hugged him.

"Victoria's changed," I said. "She longs for the freedom, and some days, she feels like she can't breathe."

When we reached Grace, we stopped. She placed her muzzle by my cheek and softly breathed in and out as I stroked her face. She put her muzzle to Joseph's hand and licked it.

"She remembers me!" Joseph said, laughing.

"Of course she does! Joseph, there are many people who can't accept who we are. They don't like us, because our skin is not quite light enough or because of our accents when we speak. Even Papa. He's having problems accepting that we were raised by the Blackfoot. It's taken a lot of time for him to accept that we love them."

"Would you ever go back?" Joseph asked.

"To live with the Blackfoot?"

He nodded.

"At one time I would have," I replied. "But I can't now. I'm married and have children. Their world is here."

I considered this for a moment.

"But if I hadn't married someone from outside, like Sara did, I'd have stayed. I was happy there."

"After you left," Joseph said, frowning, "I told myself that, once I got older, I'd have to leave too."

"Oh, Joseph, that isn't true. You have to do what makes sense for you. It's different for you than it was for me. You were a baby when we went to live with the Blackfoot. You've never known anything different or spoken another language, but I was older."

He nodded, and smiled.

"Today was my first time in a house!"

"A bit cramped, isn't it?"

"I felt like I'd bump into something."

"Always remember," I said, taking hold of his hand again, "you're always welcome with me, and with Victoria too. When you want to visit, don't hesitate."

Joseph and Machk spent the night with us, and left for home in the morning.

CHAPTER 15

"We're moving back to Canada," Remi told Moïse, during supper with us one night the following winter.

I looked from Remi to Martha. Her eyes shone brightly, and she pursed her lips.

Moïse whistled softly. "Are you?"

Remi nodded. "They're just opening up the North-West Territories."

Moïse nodded and glanced at me. He'd told me this earlier in the week, in passing.

"The grazing's good," Remi continued.

"I've heard that," Moïse replied, nodding. "And that there's rivers, and rolling hills, and sheltered and well-watered valleys."

Remi looked out the window at the blizzard that was raging outside.

"And the climate's ideal. They get the Chinook winds that warm up the country quickly through the winter, exposing the grass below. And they're building up the police too. We can sell them our horses."

"Who's going?" Moïse asked.

"Most of us. The Mongeons, LeBoeufs, Lefevres," replied Remi, counting families off on his fingers. "Why don't you come too?"

I looked over at Moïse. He had a thoughtful look on his face.

"There's money to be made in cattle," Remi declared, nodding his head. "They've developed new ways to preserve the meat."

"Oh?" said Moïse.

"Refrigeration," said Remi. "It'll open up markets. I'm going to buy a herd, and we'll drive them north to the good pastures up there."

I felt my heart sink. Remi glanced at me. He was a kind man, and perceptive. Appearing to sense my discomfort, he quickly changed the subject.

"Did you hear about the geese up there?" he asked, laughing.

Moïse shook his head.

"At one of the farms in the North-West, a storm blew in at harvest time. They'd harvested the oats, but the grain hadn't yet been housed and was still standing in stooks."

Remi paused as he surveyed his audience.

"Well, during this storm, hundreds of wild geese were blown to the farm and began to eat the grain. They even ate the straw!"

Moïse laughed.

"The farm boss ordered the hands to defend the crop and fight off the geese," Remi continued, "but they were outnumbered and unable to prevent the ravages of the geese."

Remi began laughing.

"Why didn't they just shoot them?" Moïse asked.

Remi held out his arms and raised his eyebrows.

Later that night, Moïse broached the subject of moving to Canada again.

"We could buy a farm."

"But we have a beautiful farm here," I said.

"Yes, but the land is just opening up in the west," Moïse pointed out. "We'll be able to get a homestead."

"But we already have one here," I repeated.

"Yes, but the grazing is better there."

"But Moïse!" I exclaimed, tears filling my eyes. "Victoria and Joseph are here, and I was only just reunited with Papa."

"Victoria is married with a child," said Moïse, trying to reassure me. "And Joseph is grown up. You saw him. He's grown into a responsible and capable young man."

"Yes, but Victoria needs me," I pleaded. "She's always needed me."

Joseph still had Koko. He'd thrive. Koko would see to it. But Victoria no longer had Koko to lean on. Victoria had indeed given birth to a little girl, whom she'd named Claira, but Victoria also still treated me like her own mother. How could I leave her?

"She'll be fine," said Moïse.

Despite my protests, he had his heart set on us moving north and began making preparations. Victoria stopped eating when I told her what Moïse was planning.

"I can't live without you," she said.

"Oh, Vic," I replied, putting my arms around her narrow shoulders.

"I'd rather go with you," she whispered.

"But you're married to a wonderful man and have a beautiful little baby girl."

I looked over at the angelic face of Claira, who lay sound asleep, swaddled in the flaps of the cradleboard. It was my gift to Victoria at the time of her baby's birth. I'd embroidered the buckskin with quills and beads formed into the shapes of flowers and butterflies.

"Yes," Victoria agreed, as she started to cry. "But I need you."

I hugged Victoria to me, and then glanced down at the sleeping Claira.

"Look!" I said, softly.

A butterfly had landed on the beaded flower and was slowly fanning its wings.

"Koko told me that they carry sleep and dreams. And Mama grew lovely flowers in the garden below the kitchen window at the farm in Iowa. The butterflies used to land and drink the nectar from the purple coneflowers."

Papa joined us for supper that night.

"What's the matter, Julia?" he asked, studying my face.

"Moïse wants to move to Canada. He wants us to go to the North-West Territories, with the other French Canadian families."

Papa nodded. "What's wrong with that?"

"I don't want to go," I replied, shaking my head and crossing my arms.

"Why?"

"My family's here."

"You mean Victoria and Joseph?"

I nodded. "And you," I added, softly.

He thought for a moment.

"Julia, you must find your own way."

I nodded.

"You have your own family to care for now. And it's your turn to play your part."

"What do you mean?"

"This is a new part of the world. It's just being formed. You have a chance to play your part in its creation."

I shook my head. "But we're doing that here."

"Yes," he said, "but this must also be done in western Canada."

"But I'm not from Canada."

"No, but I am, and both of your grandfathers were. And Moïse and all of your neighbours are."

I nodded. Papa frowned slightly, and then looked serious.

"I feel like the laws failed me here," he said. "Help build a better world, Julia, where you and your children are accepted."

It broke my heart to leave. With all of the French Canadian families moving north, François decided that he should head south towards California. He spoke at length with Moïse, who gave him the names of his brothers who now resided there. Victoria pleaded with Papa to move south too, but Papa refused. He felt content on his piece of property in Oregon.

We drove two covered wagons away from the farm. Moïse drove a four-mule wagon filled with the farm implements and household furniture, while I drove a two-horse wagon that carried Edouard and Philomène, the bedding, and the supplies for the trip. I waved to Victoria and Papa. Tears were streaming down Victoria's face, and she was wringing her hands. Papa was trying to keep his emotions under control, but finally broke down, the tears running down his face as well. He put his arm around Victoria, and her tiny frame was soon wracked with sobs.

CHAPTER 16

APRIL 1881

"He's better than any man around," Whistler boasted, tipping his head in the direction of the old black steer wearing a cowbell. "His name's Old Gus, and he doesn't even think that he's a steer!"

Whistler laughed, and then removed his hat, hitting it hard against his leg to remove the dust. "And he's been on so many drives," he added, replacing his hat, "he just knows what the men are askin'."

I studied the man, who was the new trail boss Moïse had hired to accompany us on our trip to the North-West Territory. He wore a waist belt on top of a red flannel shirt, with a knife tucked into it. A bullet pouch and powder horn hung at his side, and a rifle rested against the high pommel of his saddle, with a blanket roll secured to the back. He rode a sorrel horse and held onto the lead ropes of three horses that stood dozing behind them.

And Whistler was right. The cattle followed Old Gus. They established a pecking order within the herd as we travelled along the trail, with the weakest at the back and the strongest at the front, but no one challenged Old Gus. He also seemed to understand his importance on the drive and didn't even bed down with the cattle. Instead, each night, he'd wander into camp looking for treats.

"Can I feed him?" asked Edouard, as the steer sniffed the blanket near where he sat.

"Well, sure you can," Whistler replied, handing Edouard a piece of dried apple to give the steer. "He loves apples!"

"Where will he sleep?" Edouard asked.

"Near my bedroll," Whistler replied, laughing. "He's better than a dog!"

During the first week, we drove a string of two hundred horses, two hundred head of cattle, and a dozen mules for miles each day in order to remove them from their home range and break them to the trail.

"Otherwise, they'll just bolt for home," Whistler explained to Edouard, at the end of one particularly long day.

We left the Grande Ronde Valley and travelled through the Powder Valley, a wide expanse covered with pines trees and streams, and then through to Baker Valley and Pleasant Valley. At midday, we'd stop at a creek to water the livestock, while the children splashed and played in the creek and hunted for frogs and young turtles.

The grazing was good in these valleys. The sweet, tender spring grass was growing, and the livestock thrived and were content. The terrain was gentle and rolling through these valleys too, allowing us to make good time. By the second week though, we'd entered the Burnt River Canyon, the trail became very steep and dangerous, and we had to cut back on our daily mileage.

Our guide for the trip was Brisbana, a quiet, good-natured man who'd grown up on the prairies. His bravery was much celebrated, along with his hunting skills.

"They say he's killed more 'an thirty grizzly bears!" Whistler told us one night after supper, as he lit his pipe.

"Why are the hills so black?" I asked Brisbana,

"The grass is so dry," Brisbana explained, referring to the canyon's semi-arid environment, "that it often catches on fire, and that blackens the soil."

It took us about a week to navigate the canyon's narrow ledges and make our own way up the steep ascent out of it. Although it was a relief to move away from the narrow trail within the canyon, the terrain remained dry and the grass was sparse.

A few days later, at midday, we stopped near a wide river.

"Which river is that?" I asked Brisbana.

"The Snake," he replied, staring at the river with a look of respect. "This is Farewell Bend."

"Farewell Bend?" I said, frowning, the name sounding very ominous.

Brisbana nodded.

"It's the last glimpse that travellers have of the Snake when heading west, after miles of travelling along it."

"Will we cross it?" I asked, staring at the wide river.

"We'll cross it," he replied, scratching his whiskered chin, "but not here. We'll head south towards Vale and cross it there."

We left Farewell Bend and travelled southward into a large, flat alkali desert that was a challenge to negotiate. As the trail boss, Whistler's job was to locate a fresh water source ahead of us. He worked closely with Brisbana to map out our route, and then determined each day how long the treks would be in order to reach the water sources. Some of our drives were short, while others, particularly in an area like this that was devoid of fresh water, ended up taking more time.

"Keep 'em movin'!" Whistler called out.

He waved his arm forward as we approached another watering hole. Since leaving Farewell Bend, we'd only seen a few of them.

"But the animals need water," I called back.

My throat felt parched, and my team of horses was becoming lethargic and fatigued.

"Not at this one," he yelled, waving his arm again. "It's tainted and will make 'em awful sick."

He'd also said the same thing at the previous two holes, so the men had driven the herd hard past the water.

"We'll water 'em at Birch Creek," he called out.

"Mama!" I cried, waking from the dream with a start.

I was breathing hard. My heart was pounding, and my clothes were drenched with sweat. I tried to reassure myself.

A dream. It was only a dream.

Over time, this particular memory had faded, but the choking feeling of fear never abated.

I turned my head on the pillow, made from my bunched-up coat. I could see the sun rising on the horizon as thin ribbons of clouds rippled across it, forming a carpet of steps down which the sun would step throughout the morning, each ribbon a fainter echo of the one before it. We were camped at Birch Creek, just north of Vale, where we planned to cross the Malheur River later that day. We'd arrived late the night before. The livestock were exhausted and seemed unable to quench their thirst.

I rolled out from under the wagon where I'd slept, stood up, and stretched. The camp was still. Moïse and Whistler were asleep on their bedrolls, their horses still saddled up and tied to the wheels of the wagon near where the men slept. They'd worked the middle shift of the night watch. Based on how they lay on their bedrolls, they must have fallen asleep right after their shift.

A soft tune floated through the air. I spotted Louie and his brother Charlie walking their horses slowly past the resting cows, circling in opposite directions and throwing back any animal that worked its way out of the herd. Louie had his head tipped back as he sang a tune.

"*In the sweet, by and by*," he sang, in a clear voice.

"*We shall meet on that beautiful shore*," sang Charlie, in response.

"Why do you sing?" Edouard had asked at supper the night before.

"I don't always," Louie replied, smiling broadly. "I sometimes yodel or whistle too."

"What's a yodel?" Edouard asked.

"It's this," said Louie.

He tipped his nose into the air and sang a tune, rapidly changing his pitch from low to high and back again.

Edouard laughed.

"But why?"

"'Cuz we gotta keep a noise goin'," replied Charlie.

Edouard frowned.

"It reassures 'em," Charlie explained.

"The cows?" asked Edouard.

Louie nodded. "Otherwise, any sound will set 'em off runnin'."

"What kind of sound?" asked Edouard.

"Like a horse shakin', or a twig breakin', or you clappin' your hands," Charlie replied.

"I was on a drive once where a greenhorn struck a match on his saddle," added Louie, laughing. "The night was black, and the cows were so scared that they jumped to their feet and bolted."

Charlie laughed and slapped his thigh. "And remember when the sizzle from bacon frying set 'em off?"

"You also gotta watch if they're hungry or thirsty," Whistler added. "They get restless like, and are up and down disturbing each other. They get themselves ready to run!"

"Yup," said Louie. "If you let 'em eat and drink just before they're put onto the bed ground, they'll lie down and rest."

Thankfully, that morning the cows were lying quietly, chewing their cud and seeming to enjoy the brothers' serenade. I watched Brisbana ride out toward Charlie and Louie, and then saw Old Gus stand up from where he'd rested for the night and wander over to the men. He strutted past them then, one by one, and the cattle stood up from where they'd bedded for the night and followed Gus to the fresh piece of pasture. They'd graze for a few hours until we were ready to travel. The men followed the cattle and positioned their horses around the herd.

Before leaving the farm in Union County, Moïse had also hired two horse wranglers, Pierrot and Jacques, to tend to the large herd of horses on the trip. The boys were young, probably no older than their late teens, and were assisted by Gerry and his brother Félix, our neighbours from Oregon who were also immigrating north. They brought with them fifty of their own horses, in addition to the one hundred belonging to Moïse and me, and the saddle strings for each of the riders.

Grace and Poppy were among the horses that Moïse and I had brought with us. Moïse had tried to convince me to leave both horses at home in Union, for Victoria. I flat-out rejected this thought, since I just couldn't part with either of these mares. And each night, after the livestock were bedded down, I'd checked for heat in Grace's leg and would apply a soothing compress when she seemed to be favouring it.

I saw Pierrot sitting hunched over in his saddle. He'd worked as the nighthawk the previous night, guarding the horses from sunset until dawn as they grazed and slept. He'd soon begin driving the horses into a corral formed by heavy ropes strung between the three wagons and supported all around with forked stakes. He'd then be spelled off by Jacques.

After we'd set up camp, I started the fire, using pieces of wood that Jacques had gathered the previous day. I ground the coffee beans and put them into a large pot filled with water, which I hung over the fire. I put strips of salt pork into the frying pan over the fire, then pulled a piece of dough from the sourdough starter in the wagon, placing it next to the salt pork in the frying pan to grill.

The smell of the food and coffee slowly wafted through the camp, waking its inhabitants. Moïse, Whistler, Gerry, and Félix crawled out of their bedrolls, and the children climbed down from the wagon, where they'd slept on a mattress that was fitted into its box. While the men filled their plates with food, I handed the children warm biscuits spread with fruit preserves. Yawning and squinting in the early morning light, they sat on the ground near the fire and ate their meal.

Once the men were finished eating, they spelled off Brisbana and the men still on night watch, allowing them to eat and grab a few hours of sleep before we headed out on the trail. Lassos then whistled through the air as the men attempted to rope their first riding horses of the day. The horses stood shoulder to shoulder in the makeshift paddock with their rumps toward the men. The ropes were thrown from waist height in an effort to keep the horses as calm as possible. Despite these efforts, the horses jostled and dodged the ropes.

"Does it matter which horse you ride?" I'd asked Louie one morning, as he attempted to rope a horse that evaded his numerous efforts.

"Well, sure it does," he'd replied, adjusting his hat and rubbing a cloth over the sweat at the back of his neck. "Some of my horses have long legs and are good for travellin' long distances. Others have good eyesight, a good sense of direction, and are calm, which makes 'em good for night herdin.'"

The men changed out their horses again at midday in order to avoid over-riding each horse. But the ones that Moïse and I had brought with us on the trip were different. They were bred to run and most of them were still green, with no experience on the trail or pulling a wagon. All our horses had been handled extensively from birth, so although they weren't difficult to catch, many of them hadn't previously been bridled or hitched up to a wagon. In order to prevent the small number of seasoned horses that we'd brought from breaking down, each day an experienced horse and a green horse were hitched to my wagon. On some days, hitching the green horse would be done very quickly. On other days, Moïse would end up soaked with sweat from the fight that ensued.

Once hitched to the wagon, my work would begin, but I was always amazed at how much the horses learned from each other. By the end of the drive each day, the green horse was broken to driving, so each morning, Moïse would hitch up a different team. Gradually, our herd of racing horses became broken to driving.

My team that day was a good one. Buck was a seasoned driving horse. He was a beautiful buckskin colour, strong, surefooted, and very eager to listen. His mouth felt soft and his ears were constantly flicking back and forth as he listened to my commands. My second horse was a big black gelding named Ben. He had a placid temperament and quietly let Moïse catch him and tack him up. Ben was inexperienced at driving, so felt stiffer than Buck, but was very willing and took his cues from his partner. I was soon lulled into a feeling of complacency with this team. They walked forward quietly over the flat, albeit bumpy ground, and I became lost in conversation with my children, who rode on a mattress in the back of my wagon.

I soon learned that there was a particular order to the drive. My place was directly behind Brisbana, and the herd of horses followed me. Moïse's, and Gerry and Félix's wagons were positioned after the horses, followed by the cattle. The other men had specific roles along the trail. Some rode in front of the livestock, some at the back, and some along the sides in order to keep the animals moving forward and prevent them from straying.

"Tell us a story, Mama," Philomène asked.

"What do you want to hear about?" I replied, holding the slack reins in my hands.

"About when you were a little girl," said Philomène, clapping her hands.

"Well," I began, "I was born on a big farm in Iowa, where we grew wheat, had an apple orchard, and raised cows, horses, and chickens. And we stored our fruit and vegetables in a cave carved into the hills behind our house."

"What was it like?" Edouard asked.

"It was cool and dark. I remember walking up to it in the winter with Mama, then sliding all the way down the hill on our way back to the house."

"On a sled?" asked Edouard.

"Yes," I replied, smiling back at him. "Grand-Papa built us one. He also built our house and the barn."

Suddenly, I heard a sharp whinny and felt the reins being pulled through my fingers. I scrambled and grabbed hold of them again, sliding my fingers up the leather to remove the slack.

"Whoa!" I called out to Buck and Ben, pulling back on the reins. "Walk! Whoa!"

But they didn't listen. I tugged on the reins again. There was a bit of give on Buck's side, but it felt as if Ben had clamped down on the bit with his jaw and was resisting me. I braced my foot against the board in front of me, pulling back on the reins, but it was no use. I tried turning Buck, but wasn't strong enough to fight against the galloping horses.

I glanced over and saw Gerry racing up alongside them.

"Lie down!" I yelled to the children in the back of the wagon.

Gerry manoeuvred his horse so that it was beside Buck and then grabbed the reins and began pulling Buck towards him as he slowly turned his own horse. Gradually, the wagon began moving in a big circle and my team slowed down, as did the herd of horses that began galloping behind my wagon.

Once the wagon was stopped, Brisbana rode back to me.

"You okay?" he asked.

I was breathing hard and could feel my heart pounding in my chest. I glanced back at the children, who were crying in the back of the wagon, and nodded at Brisbana. I saw him glance suspiciously at the surrounding terrain.

"We'll break here for midday," he said.

"What happened?" I asked.

"He was spooked by a brave shaking a blanket," he replied, pointing to a nearby bluff.

I stared at him in horror.

"Shoshone," he said.

I nervously scanned the bluffs. Undoubtedly, there would be more than one brave, and they would be watching our every move. This felt too much like that day many years ago, when I was travelling west with Mama and Papa.

"What do we do?" Moïse asked, during our midday meal.

"Give them gifts," replied Brisbana.

"Will it help?" Moïse asked.

Brisbana nodded. "They'll probably leave us alone."

"Let's turn around, Moïse," I said, quietly.

"We can't; I sold the farm," replied Moïse softly, taking hold of my hand. "They're probably just warning us to stay off this land, or maybe they wanted to cause a stampede and make off with the scattered animals. Let me try talking to them."

I pursed my lips as he stood up.

"How will you know where to go?" I asked.

"Brisbana knows. He's done this before."

"But what if something happens to you?" I said, remembering what had happened to Mama.

"Nothing will happen to me," he said, shaking his head, and then took hold of my shoulders and looked me in the eye. "But if I don't return, continue."

I inhaled sharply.

"Go on to Canada with Gerry and Félix," he continued. "The other families will take care of you."

"Oh, Moïse," I replied, tears welling in my eyes, as I hugged him tightly.

We'd agreed to move the rest of the livestock to Vale, where we'd wait for their return before crossing the Malheur River. I watched the men ride away, carrying with them gifts of tea and tobacco.

What if he doesn't come back?

CHAPTER 17

The water was warm in the Malheur River at Vale. It was heated by the nearby hot springs, and after two weeks on the trail, everyone and everything that we owned was covered in dust. So, while we waited for the men's return, I washed the clothing and bedding while the children splashed and played in the water. Every time I heard a noise, I'd scan the horizon, looking for Moïse, but by suppertime, there was still no sign of him or Brisbana.

"Something's wrong," I told Whistler, as I pushed my food around on my plate.

"Nah," he said, while spooning beans into his mouth. "They'll be fine."

Whistler turned out to be a blessing on this trip. Nothing seemed to suppress his cheerfulness, whether long hours in the saddle, obstinate animals, heat, or fatigue. And at night, he'd sit by the fire, smoke his pipe, and tell stories that kept everyone in good humour.

After supper, I handed a cup of coffee to Whistler.

"Thank you," he said, tipping his nose up.

"What is it?" I asked, sitting down near the fire.

I sniffed the air too, but could only smell the coffee from the cup that I held in my hands.

"Rain," he replied, nodding. "I smell rain."

I sniffed the air again and frowned. I couldn't smell anything, and the day had been clear, without a cloud in the sky.

"Yup," he added. "It's movin' in."

And sure enough, the next morning we woke up to overcast skies. The clouds hung low, but for the moment, it wasn't raining.

"We gotta move, missus," he told me as I placed a piece of sourdough into the pan to grill.

I shook my head.

"We can't," I said. "Moïse and Brisbana haven't yet returned."

"If we don't cross the river now," he warned, "it'll be too swollen to cross for a week or more. Plus, the grass here isn't good enough for the cattle. We'd have to move them anyway, and this is the best place to cross."

I frowned.

"Come take a look," said Whistler.

I followed him to the banks of the river. The level had risen substantially from the day before when I'd washed laundry and the children had splashed around in the water. The river was moving much more quickly too.

Gerry let out a low whistle, as he and Felix joined us.

"Why's it so high?" I asked.

"They must be getting' rain upstream," Whistler explained, "and the snowpack's meltin'. We've gotta get the livestock across."

He looked from me to Félix and Gerry

I shook my head, as a sense of panic welled within me. "We can't."

"We've got two rivers to cross," Whistler replied. "And this one's the smaller of the two. We'll wait for 'em on the other side of the river."

"But what if Moïse needs help?" I asked.

"He's with Brisbana," Gerry replied. "He's the best person for Moïse to be with. He grew up here."

I pursed my lips, but the men were adamant.

We began readying the wagons to cross the river. Gerry and Félix prepared a wax paste and used it to fill the open spaces between the boards of the wagons.

"Why are you doing that?" Edouard asked.

"To stop water from coming into the wagon," Gerry explained. "From between the boards."

"We gotta go now!" Whistler yelled to me, once the teams were hitched and everyone was sitting astride their horses. "I'll lead the way."

I drove my wagon into the water behind Whistler. Unlike other days during our journey, this time I had two experienced horses hitched to the wagon.

"Sit in the middle of the box," I warned Edouard and Philomène. "Don't go near the edge of the wagon."

I knew that I wouldn't be able to watch them on the crossing and couldn't chance one of them falling into the river.

Gerry drove Moïse's wagon, while Félix drove the third one and the rest of the men drove the livestock across the river. The river was deep. I could feel the water current pushing against the wagon, but we managed to cross the river with only a little bit of water seepage into the boxes. The livestock also made it safely onto the opposite bank without incident.

However, Whistler still looked agitated.

"We gotta keep goin'," he insisted.

"We can't," I replied, looking over at Gerry and Félix, who were still seated on the driver seats of the other wagons.

"We gotta get across the Snake," Whistler continued.

"How far is it from here?" asked Gerry.

"About one day's ride," Whistler replied. "We'll get there today and cross tomorrow."

"But how will Moïse find us?" I cried.

"Moïse knows the direction that we're heading," replied Félix.

"And he can move much faster than we can with these wagons and the livestock," Gerry added.

"We travelled with him from the east," said Félix, smiling. "He understands river crossings. He'll catch up with us."

So, we continued heading eastward, away from the Malheur River and across Keeney Pass. We left the rain clouds behind and felt the oppressive heat of the sun beating down on us. I'd never seen such thick dust. The livestock's feet sank deep into it and the horses had to work harder to pull wagons through fine dust. As if that wasn't enough, the wind picked up as well, making it difficult to see Whistler ahead of me. The children and I wore pieces of cloth over our noses and mouths, and I squinted my eyes to minimize the effect of the dust that seemed intent on scouring them. We plodded forward and eventually got through it, arriving at the banks of the Snake River, south of Nyssa.

Whistler had been right. The murky brown water was moving more swiftly than we'd seen at the Malheur. We stood on the west bank of the river and watched a wagon pulled by two mules enter the water from the opposite bank. The mules managed to manoeuvre in the water relatively easily, until one of them lost its footing part way across. The mule's head disappeared under water and the wagon tipped, upsetting the second mule. Then the wagon and both mules were turned upside down by the current and the animals became entangled in the harness and started thrashing about. The two men that had been driving the wagon jumped out before it tipped, and then dove under the surface in a desperate struggle to untangle the mules from their harnesses and get them ashore.

I held my hand to my mouth and watched in horror.

"What if that happens to one of our wagons?" I hushed.

"Maybe we should wait for the water to lower," Gerry said, nodding.

"That could take weeks," said Whistler, shaking his head.

"But we can't risk the wagons overturning," I added.

If something happened to us, Moïse would never know. And I remembered how horrible I'd felt, not knowing the whereabouts of my parents when I was growing up.

"We'll tie the wagons together," Whistler suggested, "and float 'em across. That way, the current can't flip 'em."

I was still sceptical but went along with their plan.

Towards evening, we heard horses galloping towards our camp. The men jumped to their feet, and I held the children close to me. The riders pulled at the reins, halting their horses; then one of the men pulled the cloth away from his nose and mouth.

"Moïse!" I called out.

"Papa!" Edouard and Philomène cried in unison, running toward him.

Moïse dismounted and caught them up in a hug, and then strode over to me and hugged me close. Once he released me, I looked at the two other men who'd accompanied him. They were Shoshone braves.

"These men will help us across," Moïse explained.

"What happened?" I asked.

"I offered the chief the tea and tobacco and was offered a seat on the ground," Moïse replied, smiling. "Then he told me, 'Go on, no trouble for you,' and sent a couple of men to pilot us across the river."

Moïse laughed.

"I didn't think that you'd find us," I said.

"As soon as I saw the Malheur," he replied, "I knew that you'd had to keep moving."

I smiled at Félix and Gerry, and turned back to Moïse.

"We saw a wagon overturn crossing the Snake today," I told him, gravely. "What if that happens to us too?"

"The Shoshone will bring a scow," Moïse explained. "They'll ferry us across."

In the morning, the Shoshone floated a large flat boat down the river to our location. The cattle were driven across the river first. Louie swam his horse across the river in front of the cattle, to help guide them across and keep them moving toward the far shore. In order to minimize the risk of drowning, Louie unsaddled his horse, and then removed his boots, jeans, and shirt, riding his horse bareback, clothed in just his undershirt and underwear. One by one, the cattle entered the water and began to swim across.

Once Louie and his horse reached the opposite shore, the wind picked up. It started to pour, and then the rain became mixed with large pieces of hail. It wasn't long before two inches of hailstones covered the shoreline.

The storm scared the cattle. They saw the ice hitting the water and began to balk at the river, refusing to enter it. The cattle arriving on the opposite shore also began milling around. They turned in a circle until they became jammed tightly together and started stepping on top of each another, forcing some of the animals under water and into the vise-like grip of the sand at the river's edge.

"The cattle!" Whistler and Moïse shouted to Louie in unison, pointing to the animals circling on the sandbar.

"Old Gus!" Whistler exclaimed.

Louie dismounted from his horse and ran back towards the cattle. He climbed up onto Old Gus and began kicking at his sides, riding him through the circling cattle and up onto the shore. This stopped the cattle circling, and they slowly began following him up onto the shore.

The storm then petered out as quickly as it had begun. The men tried herding the rest of the cattle into the river, but they balked, jumping back away from the water.

"Dammit!" said Whistler.

"What do we do?" Moïse asked.

"We need Old Gus," replied Whistler. "They don't have anyone to follow. I'll ride my horse across."

He climbed onto his horse and rode it into the river, but quickly turned back.

"It's too cold, damn it!" he cursed.

We were now in deep trouble. A soaked and half-naked Louie was on one side of the river with half of the cattle, while the remainder of the herd, the wagons with our supplies, and the horses, remained on the opposite bank.

"We could send a wagon over with some food and clothing on the scow," Moïse suggested.

"I'll go," said Félix.

"I have to go too," Whistler added. "I need to bring Old Gus back. The herd needs someone to follow across the river."

Moïse's wagon was loaded and secured with wooden blocks to stabilize it on the scow. Félix and the Shoshone braves climbed aboard the scow, followed by Whistler.

The Shoshone shook his head and said something to Brisbana.

"He says that you'll have to stay here," Brisbana told Whistler. "It's overloaded."

"No," said Whistler, adamantly, shaking his head. "I need to help bring Old Gus back."

"Félix'll put him onto the scow," said Moïse.

Whistler anxiously paced on the shore, watching as the scow made its way across the river. Félix and the wagon arrived safely on the other side of the river. Then Louie and Félix loaded Old Gus onto the scow with the Shoshone, and pushed the scow back towards our side of the river. The scow was about halfway across the river when Old Gus began snorting, shaking his head, and swishing his tail.

"Somethin's wrong," said Whistler.

"What is it?" I asked.

"He's afraid of the water," Whistler replied. "The storm's musta scared 'im. And now the sun's shinin' on the water."

He spat on the ground. The clouds had parted, and the sun was reflecting brightly off the waves on the river.

"I gotta do somethin'," said Whistler, removing his boots. "He's gonna jump."

"No!" Moïse exclaimed.

He tried grabbing Whistler's arm, but Whistler evaded him, dove into the fast-moving water, and started swimming towards the scow.

Old Gus spotted Whistler swimming towards him and spooked again, unable to identify the dark shape splashing through the water toward him. Old Gus shied to the edge of the scow and leapt into the river, away from Whistler.

CHAPTER 18

Whistler saw Old Gus jump into the water, struggling to keep his head above the surface. Whistler swam hard towards the steer and grabbed hold of him. Whistler managed to keep both of their heads above water but was unable to swim to the shore. Without hesitation, one of the Shoshone braves on the scow dove into the water and swam hard, with strong strokes, toward Whistler. The brave on the scow threw a rope and the other man in the water helped Whistler tie this around Old Gus' body, behind his front legs, preventing the current from dragging him farther downstream. Then the brave and Whistler swam to shore, pulling old Gus ashore with them and onto a sandbar that jutted out into the water.

The other men on shore ran downstream to the sandbar and pulled the men and the steer farther up onto the bank. I built up the fire and put on a fresh pot of coffee before bringing out more blankets to wrap around the men's shoulders when they arrived back at camp.

Whistler sat beside the fire, near where the Old Gus lay not moving.

"I don't know if he'll make it," Whistler murmured, his mouth moving stiffly.

He blinked his eyes quickly and pulled the blanket tighter around his shoulders. I handed the men steaming cups of coffee and placed a blanket over the black steer, stroking his face.

"I think that he's just exhausted," I said. "And chilled."

The fire soon dried off the men's clothing, and they began to warm up. Old Gus rolled from a flat-out position on the ground to sit upright, with his legs tucked underneath him so that he could see what was going on in the camp.

"Can I feed him something?" Edouard asked.

I nodded and smiled.

"Why not give him a piece of dried apple," I suggested, handing him a piece, looking up at Whistler for approval.

Whistler beamed and nodded.

"Me too! Me too!" Philomène called, excitedly.

Edouard held out the piece of apple to Old Gus, who sniffed it, then took it into his mouth and chewed the sweet treat. He swallowed the morsel, and then looked for more. I placed a piece of apple onto Philomène's outstretched hand, and she offered the apple to the steer. He eagerly took the treat and then licked her hand. Philomène squealed with delight.

Whistler laughed. "Well, look at that!"

The next morning, we crossed the river. Although the water level hadn't dropped, the temperature was more tolerable. We drove the cattle across the river with Old Gus in the front, and Charlie on his horse in front of Gus, leading the way across the river. The horses were then herded across, and once the wagons were ferried over the river, we thanked the braves for their help. Whistler also made a special point of shaking the hand of the brave who had rescued him and Old Gus from the river.

We followed the Goodale's Cutoff, a spur trail that ran north of the Oregon Trail from Fort Boise and through the Camas Prairie. The terrain was dry and devoid of trees.

"There was fighting here, a few years back," Brisbana explained.

"Why?" I asked, looking around at the nearby bluffs.

"Camas grow here," he explained. "And the Bannocks have dug them up for years, since it's part of their diet. But when the settlers arrived, they ran their pigs on these fields and the pigs rooted up the camas."

The days were long as we travelled through the desolate, arid landscape.

"I'm nine now," Edouard declared one day, when he was riding Grace alongside the wagon.

I nodded. "Yes, you are."

"I want to help watch the cattle at night," he said, looking pointedly at me. "Whistler thinks that I'm a good enough rider."

"Does he now?" I answered, dryly, looking at the back of Whistler, who was riding ahead of us alongside Brisbana.

"Uh-huh," Edouard replied, seriously. "He said that I could help him tonight."

After crossing the Snake River, I'd agreed to let Edouard work in the drag position, at the back of the cattle herd. Although this was very dusty, I'd thought that this would be relatively safe, since he'd only be responsible for pushing the cattle forward. But night duty? I looked back at him in horror.

That night, we'd stopped later in the day than we'd hoped. Whistler had ridden ahead, trying to locate a good water source, but by mid-afternoon, he'd ridden back toward the herd shaking his head.

"Nothing up ahead," he called back to us. "We'll have to let the cattle find it!"

"Will this work?" I called to Moïse.

He smiled and nodded. "They've got good noses for water."

And it did work. Old Gus, and the other cattle in the front of the herd, chose the direction that we should travel. After a few hours, they led us to a small creek where we ended up camping for the night.

"*Home, home on the range,*" Louie sang, in a clear voice.

"*Where the deer and the antelope play,*" sang Charlie.

"Why are they singing?" asked Philomène, as I fixed her long, dark brown hair into a thick braid down the middle of her back.

The campfire outside the wagon cast an eerie glow of continuously moving shadows on the inside of the white canvas. I closed my eyes, trying to block out a vision of a face covered in black streaks of paint. Inhaling deeply, I opened my eyes.

"They're singing to the cows," I replied, softly.

Philomène turned around and looked at me, then giggled.

"The cows?" she said, then crawled under the covers on the mattress.

I nodded and smiled.

"The cows like music. It keeps them calm."

"I like it too."

"Good night, Lady P," I said, kissing the tip of her nose.

"Moo," she replied, yawning, then giggled at her own joke. "Tell me a story, Mama."

"What would you like to hear?"

"Tell me about when you were a little girl."

"Okay. Close your eyes."

I waited until she'd pulled the covers up to her chin and closed her eyes.

"When I was a little girl, I lived on a farm," I began.

"In Iowa!" Philomène added.

"Yes, in Iowa. Our farm was nestled against large hills."

"Grand-Papa built caves in the hills!"

"Yes, and we stored potatoes, carrots, apples, and cabbages in the cave."

"Tell me about Grand-Mama."

I felt a lump form in my throat. I swallowed hard, and then smiled at her, my eyes moist.

"She was a kind woman, with long, thick hair like yours," I said, as Philomène beamed.

"And she loved to sing."

She yawned.

"Sing to me, Mama."

"Close your eyes," I said, softly, and began singing the song that my mother used to sing to me.

> *"Fais dodo, mon petit Pierrot,*
> *J' t'apprendrai à filer la laine,*
> *Fais dodo, mon petit Pierrot,*
> *J' t'apprendrai à fair' des sabots."*

I glanced up and saw that Philomène was breathing deeply. Then I crawled out of the wagon. I looked over to where Edouard was sleeping on Moïse's bedroll, near the wheel of the wagon. Grace was saddled up and stood tied to the wheel. Edouard was on guard work with Whistler that night. They'd keep an eye on the herd beginning at midnight and were asleep now in order to be alert later. I thought that Edouard was too young to take on such responsibility, but Moïse didn't agree.

"Whistler's the best person to learn from," Moïse told me.

"But he's too young," I replied.

"He has to start sometime."

On the horizon, the night was repeatedly lit up by bolts of lightning that zigzagged across the sky. Then the breeze picked up, and the air began to smell damp. I drew my shawl tighter around my shoulders.

"Will we get that storm?" I asked quietly, taking a seat by the fire next to Moïse.

I poured two cups of coffee, then handed him one.

"Not sure," he replied, glancing over at the horizon.

The cattle were becoming antsy and wouldn't bed down. Louie, Charlie, Gerry, and Félix were trying to quiet them, singing and whistling, but the cattle ignored their efforts, seeming to be just waiting for an excuse to run.

Suddenly, there was a booming crash of thunder that felt as if it rocked the ground. At the same time, a blinding flash of light almost seemed to split open the dark night sky. Then the wind howled and the cattle bolted.

Moïse leapt to his feet.

"Whistler!" he bellowed.

He ran toward his horse, which was tied to the wheel of the wagon. The horse was dancing back and forth. There was another crash of thunder, and the horse began pulling back against the slipknot tied to the wagon wheel, making it difficult for Moïse to untie. He finally yanked the rope hard, and the horse flew back. Moïse was pulled sharply forward but got a foothold and resisted the horse's backward movement. The horse stopped pulling against the rope but continued fidgeting from one foot to another.

Moïse quickly stepped his left foot into the stirrup, and threw his right leg up and over the horse's back. There was a bolt of lightning just as he lowered himself into the saddle, and the horse shot off at a gallop.

The low rumbling noise of the running cattle had awakened Whistler. He was already astride his horse and galloping with the other riders to try to get ahead of the cattle before they scattered.

Edouard was desperately pulling on Grace's slipknot. I ran over to him and grabbed his arm.

"No, Edouard. Leave her," I shouted. "You have to stay here."

"I've gotta help," Edouard cried, tugging unsuccessfully at the knot.

He pulled his hat down firmly on his head and turned his collar up to stop some of the water from running down the back of his neck.

"No, you can't!" I replied, scrambling towards the shelter of the wagon and pulling him with me.

"But, Mama!" Edouard cried, pulling his arm away from me.

"What?" I shouted.

He pointed in the direction of the stampeding cattle and horses. Then there was another boom of thunder and a bolt of lightning that seemed to split the heavens in two.

"Take cover!" I exclaimed.

Edouard scrambled into the wagon, and I dove in after him as another wave of rolling thunder rocked the ground. A further bolt of lightning lit up the inside of the wagon, illuminating Philomène. She was sitting up in bed with her hands over her ears, crying hysterically.

"Mama!" she cried when she saw me, crawling up onto my lap for reassurance.

"It's okay," I said, rocking her gently.

"I gotta help!" said Edouard, angrily.

I shook my head.

"You'd be galloping in the dark. There are cut banks and prairie dog holes all around. I can't risk you getting hurt."

There was another crash of thunder, and the wagon lit up again.

"Why does it thunder?" Philomène asked, between her sobs.

"My grandmother told me that it was a big black bird that swooped down from the sky with roaring wings," I explained, smiling faintly. "And it created lightning by flapping its wings over a lake."

"How do they stop the cattle?" Edouard asked.

"They have to gallop ahead of them and turn the lead cows, circling them back in toward the other cattle. The others will follow the leaders into a circle; then the riders will drive them into a smaller and smaller circle."

"Will they lose some of them?" asked Edouard.

I nodded. "They might."

But luckily, this time, we didn't. The men returned with the livestock several hours later. The storm had moved off, and the thunder could no longer be heard, but the sky on the horizon continued to light up periodically for a while. The night guard had to be particularly vigilant while watching the livestock.

"We gotta watch 'em close," Louie told Moïse. "Now that they've run once, they'll want to do it again."

The watch was longer that night. Instead of the usual two guards riding through the night, this was increased to three. As a result, each shift lasted longer. Edouard had long since fallen asleep and was left in peace that night.

It took us almost three weeks to get through the Goodale's Cutoff, after which we headed northeast toward Montana. The farther north we travelled, the shorter the grass became, and the more it seemed like winter. Then one morning, we woke up to a blizzard. It wasn't particularly cold, but there was a biting wind and the snow was wet and heavy.

"We gotta find cover," Whistler told Brisbana.

We began moving, but the cattle soon became stuck in snow-drifts and panicked. The men were continually roping one cow out and trying to calm it down just as another one would get stuck. I pulled my hat down over my eyes to protect them from the snow that was driving into my face. I could barely see ten yards ahead of me.

We came to a fork in the road and couldn't see which trail to follow. While we were stopped, trying to figure out which direction to turn, Old Gus sauntered up from behind the wagons and horses, and then continued past us and down one of the paths.

"We'll follow him," Whistler shouted, into the wind.

So, we followed Old Gus and within the hour we reached a ridge covered with big evergreen trees, sheltered from the wind and snow. We stayed in the shelter until the snow squall passed.

Gradually, the snow-covered trails melted, revealing lush spring grass that the half-starved livestock thrived on. A drowsy, spring-like headiness filled the air and the voices of birds, thousands of young frogs, and a multitude of insects rose up from the creeks and the meadows, pausing when we passed close by and then rising again in a chorus after we'd gone.

After about two months on the trail, we reached the town of Butte. Moïse, Gerry, and Félix ventured into town to pick up supplies from the grocery store. The rest of us remained with the livestock and wagons on the outskirts of the town.

"It's so busy," Moïse told us, when he returned.

He'd brought flour, tea, coffee, sugar, tobacco, and a sweet cake from the bakery.

"Why?" I asked.

"Mining," he replied. "They've had gold and silver mines here for years, but now they've found copper too."

"And there's lots of smoke in the air," Félix added, pointing to the pall of smoke that could be seen in the distance.

"His name's Tam O'Shanter," Moïse told Félix and Gerry.

They were sitting near the fire, sipping on their cups of steaming coffee and enjoying a slice of sweet cake. Moïse was reading from the newspaper that he'd brought back from the town.

"A trotting horse, by Mountain Chief," Moïse whistled.

"How big?" Gerry asked.

"Says over sixteen hands," Moïse read. "And listen to this, an American-bred horse named Iroquois won the Epsom Derby in England, beating the favourite, Peregrine, by a neck. Wouldn't that be something?"

The next day, we travelled northeast towards Helena and then on to Great Falls. When we set out, the weather was beautiful. The daytime temperature was pleasant, and at night, although it remained cool, it was no longer below freezing. Then one afternoon, there was a low muttering of thunder in the distant mountains and dense black masses of clouds rose ominously behind the broken peaks. Soon, the thick blackness covered the entire sky, enveloping the landscape with a deep gloom, before a gust of wind arrived. Suddenly the storm broke, lashing out with a whirling sheet of rain, forcing us to make camp.

The men pitched tents in an effort to provide some reprieve from the onslaught of rain. Throughout the night, the storm continued to pelt the landscape with rain, while the thunder bellowed and growled above our heads.

And then it stopped and there was blessed silence. In the morning, we awoke to clear blue skies, without a breath of wind. As the sun rose in the morning sky and beat down upon the landscape, the heat became almost oppressive with high humidity as the dampness evaporated.

We only crept along, as the animals waded fetlock-deep through the mud. By midday, dark masses of clouds began to form again over the mountain peaks, contrasting sharply with the brilliant sunshine that filled the landscape. Soon the wind picked up again.

"We gotta stop!" Whistler yelled, over the fevered pitch of the wind.

No sooner had the tents been pitched than the entire sky was shrouded in inky black clouds, the thunder was rumbling, and the smell of rain filled the cool air. The sheets of rain then began to fall. I climbed into the back of the wagon with the children and drew the ends of the canvas closed tight. The canvas helped to stop the rain from entering directly, but it still beat through the canvas in a fine drizzle that wet us just as much.

"I wish that we could go back home," Philomène smiled, glumly.

"Me too," I said, stroking her damp hair.

Moïse kept reassuring me that it was the rainy season and this wouldn't last, but the days were becoming long. We still had another month to go until we reached the North-West Territory. The children had been very good but were getting very restless, particularly Philomène. At least Edouard could get out and ride Grace, but Philomène was still too young to ride or walk beside the wagon. She had to be cooped up in the back of the wagon for the entire journey.

"I miss Aunt Victoria," she said.

"So do I," added Edouard.

"Me too," I said, smiling sadly. "I wonder how she's doing?"

"I bet that she's missing us as much as we are her," Edouard replied.

"I miss Claira too," Philomène sighed. "She was fun to play with."

Around sunset, the storm stopped as suddenly as it had begun, and a beautiful reddish-pink sky appeared above the western edge of the horizon. As the rays of the setting sun streamed across the prairie, thousands of mini rainbows could be seen through the droplets of water that covered the landscape.

The reprieve was short-lived. Night had scarcely set in when we were assaulted again. Flashes of lightning lit up the landscape, and the crashes of thunder boomed overhead as we were assaulted by a torrent of rain.

By morning, the worst of the storm seemed to be over and only sprinkles of rain continued to patter against the wagon's canvas. I climbed out, feeling damp and chilled to the bone. The sky was still dark with grey clouds, but these were broken up and the promise of sunshine was present in the early morning sky.

By noon, the sky was clear and we set out again, trailing through mud that was at least six inches deep. This pattern of weather continued over the course of a few weeks. The mornings were sunny and oppressively hot and humid. By afternoon, the air would cool, and large black thunderheads would appear over the mountains and then cover the sky, pelting us with rain. Then overnight, the rain would stop and we'd awake to brilliant sunshine.

And then one day, the water tap abruptly turned off and the trails became dry and dusty again.

CHAPTER 19

"Liquor and chewing tobacco," Whistler told me.

As if on cue, he spat chewing tobacco juice onto the ground beside where he sat near the fire. I wrinkled my nose.

He removed his hat, scratched at his hair, and then replaced his hat and continued.

"Red pepper, Jake, and molasses," he said, guffawing. "Yup, the last swig in the keg'll kill ya."

"What's Jake?" I asked.

"Jamaica ginger," replied Whistler, laughing. "The stuff'll paralyze you!"

"And people drink it?" I asked.

"Yes, ma'am. It's called Birch Creek Rot Gut! And it's big business!"

Whistler laughed again. I frowned, and turned my attention back to the stew I was preparing. Earlier that day, we'd passed a farmhouse, where we purchased some vegetables, a few chickens, and some eggs. Then we'd decided to break early. I added chopped carrots to the stew, along with the wild onions I'd found growing near the creek, then stirred the mixture. We'd travelled past Cut Bank and were now heading northwest towards the line into Canada.

"'Bout ten years back, the US government began crackin' down on the sale of liquor to the Indians," Whistler rambled on. "But it didn't stop the traders. Why, they just moved their whiskey north, to where the American lawmen had no authority."

"But why didn't the police in Canada stop them?" I asked, tasting the broth.

Whistler shrugged. "There weren't any."

"No police?" I asked.

He shook his head. "The only people here were the fur traders and the Indians. It's only now that they're just startin' to set up police barracks and are tryin' to stop 'em."

"How do they carry the whiskey here?" I asked.

"Pack trains."

Whistler spat more tobacco juice to his side and continued.

"The horses have kegs slung over their backs, one on each side."

"Whistler!" Moïse called out, sharply.

I looked up to where Moïse sat on horseback several hundred feet away. He was pointing to three men who were riding toward the camp.

Whistler jumped to his feet and ran to his horse. He untied it from the wagon wheel, where it stood saddled, and leapt up onto the saddle. He rode out to join Moïse and Gerry, who were riding out towards the men.

"Who are they?" Edouard asked, running to stand next to me.

Brisbana rode his horse up near where we stood.

"Blackfoot," he said.

"Quick, get into the wagon," I told Edouard. "Get Philomène too."

"But Mama!" Edouard cried. "Why? Who are they?"

"Now, Edouard! Get inside!" I repeated, pointing at the wagon.

In the distance, I saw Moïse turn his head and point in my direction. I could see him nodding and smiling at one of the men. Then they all turned their horses and began walking toward the camp. Brisbana rode out to meet Moïse. They spoke briefly, and then Brisbana rode his horse back toward the cattle.

At the camp, the men dismounted and Moïse and one of them began walking toward me. Moïse spoke to him in Blackfoot. I stared at the man and frowned. He looked familiar.

"Julia," said Moïse, smiling at me. "You remember Aranck?"

I caught my breath. He was my captor. The fear that I'd felt that night when our camp was ambushed and I was captured came flooding back. Seeming to sense this, Moïse put his arm protectively around me.

"Hello," said Aranck, smiling nervously.

I pursed my lips, and looked up at Moïse, who smiled.

I looked back at Aranck.

"Hello," I said quietly, then turned and busied myself with the stew.

The men later joined us for our meal.

"A war party's moving this way," Aranck explained.

"Moving this way?" said Brisbana, frowning.

"It's a war party. Bloods and Peigans," Aranck continued. "They're after the Cree."

"Why?" Moïse asked.

"The Cree stole horses from them," Aranck replied.

"How many men?" Brisbana asked.

"Three or four hundred," said Aranck, looking serious.

Brisbana whistled under his breath.

"All braves," Aranck continued. "And ready to fight."

"Will we be safe?" Moïse asked.

Aranck shook his head. "They'll take your horses. Especially fine horses like these."

"What should we do?" asked Moïse.

"Ride north," Aranck suggested. "Hide them in the coulees near Whiskey Gap until the party passes by."

"How far away are they?" Brisbana asked.

"Maybe a day or two," replied Aranck.

After the meal, we headed north towards Whiskey Gap and found ourselves in a labyrinth of ravines and coulees that ran in every direction.

"Best kinda protection for a rum runner!" Whistler chuckled as we entered a steep-sided, flat-floored coulee.

We split the cattle and horses up into different coulees, and waited.

Aranck and the other Blackfoot men travelled with us and acted as our sentries. They planned to negotiate with the war party if our paths crossed. The next day, the men spotted the war party. They moved off farther to the east, far enough away not to notice us.

Before leaving, Aranck sat down with Moïse and me.

"How is Sara?" I asked him.

"She's doing well," Aranck replied, smiling. "After Joseph returned from visiting you at your farm, she pestered him with questions about you and your children."

I smiled. "And Joseph?"

"He will be married soon."

Tears filled my eyes and a sense of longing tugged at my heart. Moïse reached out and stroked my back.

"Who is he marrying?" I asked.

"Petah."

I smiled again. I remembered Petah as a small child. She was few years younger than Joseph.

"And Koko?" I asked, holding back my tears at the mention of her.

"She's doing well. She missed you greatly, after you left."

He paused and glanced at me, and then frowned and turned away. He turned back to me and cleared his throat.

"I'm sorry, Julia."

I stared at him, noticing the pained look on his face.

"You have no idea," he continued, "how I've regretted taking you that day. Away from your parents."

I nodded, tears filling my eyes.

"It's haunted me," he said, swallowing hard. "Seeing you suffer as a small child."

He shook his head, and I wiped my tears.

"Thank you," I whispered then cleared my throat. "I used to be so angry, and hurt, and sad."

I put my hand to my mouth, as Moïse stroked my back softly.

"But Koko was also a wonderful mother," I said nodding, accepting that it was time to move on. "Please give my love to Joseph and Koko."

Aranck smiled at me. There were tears in his eyes.

CHAPTER 20

The wind was incessant, blowing for days on end with little reprieve. Perhaps this was the price we had to pay for the panorama of mountains, hills, and rivers that spread out before us. Some days, I had to squint my eyes shut to stop the tears that the wind brought to them, looking away from the prevailing west wind to gasp for a breath of air. But when the strong breeze blew itself out, the early morning sun cast the tips of the mountains in soft hues of pink and gold. As the sun slowly swept downward and washed the foothills and valleys in pale light, I was convinced that this corner of the Earth must resemble a piece of heaven.

I'd come to know these magnificent peaks and their legends. Chief Mountain lay to the south, the figure of the Sleeping Indian resting on the mountains, along with the trembling Turtle Mountain, and the Crow's Nest Mountain visible through the pass. We'd said our goodbyes to Whistler, Brisbana, and the others, and then joined ten other French Canadian families in a district five miles northwest of the village of Pincher Creek that would later be known as French Flats. After three months on the trail, we'd finally arrived at our destination, but this hardly meant that our work was finished. Instead, Moïse and I began the search for a homestead.

Spring had arrived late that year, and by all accounts, it had been a cold one. Following our arrival, we were subjected to one hailstorm after another, pelting ice down at us, leaving in its wake a litter of snow on the fields and a cool feel to the summer air. And then, as if that wasn't enough to cast a feeling of doubt into the minds of the newcomers, we were challenged by an early frost that snuffed the life out of the few shrubs and trees that could survive in the harsh environment.

We found a homestead nestled in the foothills southwest of Pincher Creek, where Moïse, Edouard, and a few of the other men began felling trees. They chopped them into specific lengths, flattened the wood on opposite sides, and dovetailed them into each other. Light poles were cut for the roof, overlaid with branches, and topped with sod. A gumbo was mixed up and the spaces between the logs were chinked to seal them.

But the house wasn't ready in time, and we had to live in our covered wagon during our first winter in the area. Although we'd wrapped hides of furs around the wagons, it was still very cold. When we did finally move into our new log home in the early spring, it felt wonderful.

In the beginning, the North-West Mounted Police regularly patrolled the area on horseback or buckboard. And since there wasn't yet a post office in Fort Macleod, the police picked up the mail that arrived by freight and delivered it to the various homesteads when they patrolled the area.

After our arrival the previous summer, Moïse had sent a letter to Papa in Union, notifying him that we'd arrived safely. After many months, I received a reply.

"Victoria had another baby girl," Moïse read out loud to me.

"Another baby!" I exclaimed, clasping my hands together.

"She called her Sadie Julia."

I smiled. "I hope that she's happy."

He smiled at me. "I'll write back to let him know that you're pregnant."

The following November, my son Emory was born. At the time of his birth, there was no snow. We'd had a snowstorm at the beginning of October that year, but all the snow had soon melted and very little fell after that. As we neared the end of November though, the temperatures plummeted and we found ourselves in the midst of a deep chill with no reprieve until the middle of February. Then spring finally arrived, accompanied by warmer temperatures.

"They're taking a chance," said Moïse, shaking his head when he arrived back home from a trip to Fort Macleod. "Some of the ranchers are ploughing their fields and sowing crops."

I looked over at him from where I was standing at the kitchen table kneading bread dough.

"It's March," he explained, shaking his head again. "In like a lamb, out like a lion."

And true to the saying, towards the end of the month, a snowstorm blew in that lasted for ten days and brought with it heavy, wet snow.

On one particularly blustery morning, Moïse walked back into the house, slamming the door shut.

"Five more!" he growled. "They're freezing as soon as they hit the snow."

I felt sick. We were in the middle of calving season and it seemed as if the calves were either dying from being born onto snow or dying alongside their mothers, who were starving to death, unable to paw through the deep snow to reach the grass below. I felt helpless. We didn't have anything to feed them. Why would we need hay when we had vast open fields?

On one particularly bad day, after about a week of being constantly bombarded with snow and howling winds, I heard a chirping sound as I walked past a grove of cottonwood trees near the house. I looked around but couldn't see a bird nearby. The sound continued and seemed to be coming from an oddly shaped stone near the base of a tree. I stooped down and picked up the stone, turned it over, and then grasped it tightly to my chest and ran for home.

"Moïse!" I called out, running into the house.

"What is it?"

He rushed towards me, followed by the children.

"A buffalo stone!" I cried happily, holding out the stone.

"What's a buffalo stone?" he asked, picking up the stone and turning it over in his hand.

I removed my coat and boots, and warmed myself near the fire before telling him the story that Koko had taught me many years earlier.

"It's a powerful stone that brings its finder good luck," I began, smiling. "The first buffalo stone was found many years ago, during a winter when the snow was deep and the buffalo seemed to disappear. A young woman heard singing near a cottonwood tree. The singing stopped and she spotted a stone jammed into a tree, along with a few buffalo hairs. She picked it up, and the I-nis'kim told her to take it to her tipi and sing the song that she'd heard. She should also pray that her people would not starve and that the buffalo would come back."

"What's I-nis'kim?" Philomène asked.

"The buffalo stone," I replied, and then continued. "The woman took the stone back to her home and taught her people the song that she'd heard. They prayed and soon heard the loud rumble of a large herd of buffalo in the distance, their prayers answered."

"Will you pray for buffalo?" asked Edouard, frowning.

I shook my head.

"No, for the animals."

I grasped the stone tightly in my hands and prayed that the livestock would make it through the rest of the storm without starving. After ten days, the snow stopped and the storm passed, leaving in its wake muddy roads and swollen creeks. Ironically, there had been little or no loss of life amongst the cattle in the district over the course of the winter, but during the late March storm, many of the cows and calves perished. Even a policeman travelling from Standoff to Fort Whoop-up was lost in the storm. When he was found, not only was he severely frostbitten, but both he and his horse were also snow-blind.

The winter of 1883 wasn't much better. In November, Moïse arrived back from Fort Macleod in a temper.

"There's no snow between Macleod and Pincher Creek," he barked, storming in through the door. "But look at it here!" He pointed through the open door. "We've got four inches of the damn stuff!"

The snow remained throughout the winter, once again making it difficult for the cattle to push it aside with their noses to the grass below. I grasped my buffalo stone and prayed. My prayers were answered, but this time in the form of a new homestead.

Moïse found an old outpost of the Hudson's Bay Company at the confluence of the Oldman River and the Pincher Creek, below the Brocket reservation. It was located about fifteen miles east of our first home in the area and was owned by William Samuel Lee. He'd moved to the outpost in 1870, and operated it for the Hudson's Bay Company before transporting cattle and horses up from Montana onto the property.

"The west wind'll blow the snow off the face of the hills," said Moïse. "The livestock will always have access to the grass below."

"And we'd never be short of water," I added.

In the spring of 1884, we sold our property to the Alberta Ranch Company, along with one hundred and fifty horses to Robert Duthie, the manager of the ranch. We bought Lee's outpost and moved into a twenty-foot by sixty-foot, two-storey frame house that was sheltered by a grove of trees on the north and west sides. The house was set higher than the creek; out of the flood plain, but close enough to make the creek accessible. There was a milk house, cowshed, granary, chicken house, and hog pen. In our first year, we broke and farmed over twenty-six acres, raising substantial herds of cattle, horses, and pigs.

The property was ideally located for crossing the Oldman River. Although the river was deep and swift, at this location it widened out, becoming shallower and not as fast flowing. Over time, travellers on the lonely trail between Fort Macleod and Pincher Creek used the crossing more and more. These travellers would often stop overnight or take refuge, enjoying a meal and conversation. The property also became the rendezvous of the horsemen who were keen to place wagers on their racehorses. There was always laughing and dancing, with music supplied by Moïse on the fiddle, and sometimes a Jew's harp or even a paper-wrapped comb.

Just before Christmas, in 1885, our third son Alexandre Joseph was born during a blustery cold snap, when the ice crystals fluttered to and fro outside the window and a blanket of snow carpeted the ground. However, this didn't stop our neighbours from visiting us on Christmas Day.

The North-West Mounted Police also regularly held dances at their barracks in Fort Macleod, inviting everyone in the district. These were formal affairs. The police officers sported red tunics, the women wore fancy gowns, and the civilian men wore their Sunday best. While their dances lasted, the police conveniently ignored the unmistakable odour of liquor in the air. Then after their dances ended, the officers would spill over to our dance.

And as the officers entered the large barn that we used for the dance, Moïse and Edouard joined me at a small grouping of chairs near the back of the barn, where I sat softly rocking Alexandre as he slept. Moïse and Edouard both carried the fiddles they'd played during the dance. Moïse softly kissed the top of my head, running his finger over Alexandre's soft cheek, and took a seat beside me.

Remi soon joined us, carrying a comb covered with a piece of paper, as he wiped his brow.

"Did you hear about Lamoureaux and them?" Remi asked, tilting his head in the direction of a group of men wearing red tunics.

Moïse smiled at his long-time friend and shook his head. "Is he at it again?" he asked, smoothing the hairs on his large moustache.

Remi chuckled.

"He's even got his son helping him."

The men went back to playing music. The dances usually lasted the entire night, filled with polkas, minuets, waltzes, reels, jigs, and quadrilles. Then, in the wee hours of the morning, the partygoers would eat a breakfast of beefsteaks or game meats before departing for home by horse or wagon.

But that night was different. Since it was Christmas, whiskey had been obtained under a three-gallon limit permit, and the liquor flowed unceasingly throughout the night.

"Bet it's contraband," said an officer named Sergeant Taylor, with a smirk.

"What did you say?" Moïse asked, standing up from where he'd been sitting enjoying his plate of food.

"Nothing," the sergeant replied. "Just commenting on the whiskey." He roared with laughter and slapped his leg. The other men around him chuckled.

"Out!" Moïse snapped.

He marched over to where the sergeant sat, grabbing him by the front of his shirt. "You come to my place and make accusations like this! Out!"

The police officers left the property, but only after a fight had broken out on the dance floor, fuelled by the alcohol consumed by everyone.

"And that was necessary?" I asked Moïse the next day, when I saw the bump on his forehead.

"They accused me of having contraband alcohol," he replied, scowling. "Insulting!"

I shook my head.

A few days later, our good friend Gerry stopped by to eat supper with us. He told us the story of Staff-Sergeant Wright and Sergeant Taylor of the NWMP.

"They made a bet," said Gerry, chuckling. "Twenty-five dollars!"

"Twenty-five dollars!" Moïse echoed, whistling.

Gerry nodded.

"About who could capture Lamoureaux red-handed first."

Moïse snorted. I took three steaming cups of coffee to the table and sat down to enjoy the story. The Lamoureaux family was one of those with whom we had travelled north from Oregon.

"Taylor was patrolling Tennessee Coulee," Gerry continued. "He saw a large sleigh drawn by four galloping horses heading towards Macleod. He chased after the sleigh on his horse, but when the driver of the sleigh spotted him, he whipped his horses forward."

"Oh, no!" said Moïse, laughing.

Gerry chuckled and nodded.

"Taylor chased after the sleigh, and fired his pistol into the air."

Gerry held up his hand and pretended to pull the trigger of a gun.

"And the driver of the sleigh pulled up and stopped."

"Lamoureaux?" Moïse asked.

Gerry shook his head.

"His son!"

"Has he taken after his papa?" I asked.

Old man Lamoureaux was a character. He was a generous, kind man with a sense of humour, and he loved nothing more than to trick the authorities.

Gerry smiled and nodded. "Taylor searched the loaded sleigh, tossing out handfuls of straw to reveal half a dozen kegs! He moved a keg and heard liquid sloshing inside. He told young Lamoureaux that he was under arrest and took him into Macleod."

Moïse shook his head.

"Oh, it gets better!" said Gerry, grinning. "So, Wright had one of the kegs opened and sniffed inside."

"I bet that it was water!" Moïse laughed, and then looked over at Edouard whose eyes were wide with admiration. "Don't get any ideas, young man."

"No, sir," said Edouard, his cheeks turning pink.

"Yup!" Gerry added. "Every keg was filled with water."

Moïse burst out laughing.

"Well, Taylor was mad!" Gerry continued. "He was the laughing stock of the barracks. And of course, Wright was leading the taunts!"

Moïse chuckled.

"There's more!" said Gerry. "Then a stranger approached Taylor and struck a deal with him. In exchange for an escort across the line, he'd guide Taylor to a spot where Lamoureaux would be sure to pass."

"Who was he?" Moïse asked.

Gerry shook his head. "Not sure, but Taylor and a few men rode out with the stranger when the moon was bright and glowed off the snow. They hid behind some brush on the side of the hill. Then they waited and waited."

He paused and looked at all of us, as we listened intently.

"And then they heard the crunching of dry snow under horses' hooves, as two sleighs approached."

"Lamoureaux?" Edouard asked.

Gerry smiled and held up his finger. "And then one of the police horses neighed and was answered by one of the horses pulling the sleighs."

"Oh, no!" said Moïse, laughing.

"Well, they made a run for it," Gerry added.

"Who was in the second sleigh?" asked Edouard.

"Just wait!" Gerry replied, chuckling. "When the police caught up with the sleighs, the drivers wheeled about, dismounted, and then opened fire on the police!"

Moïse opened his eyes wide.

"A bullet killed the stranger's horse," Gerry continued. "The police managed to disarm one of the drivers, but the other took off in the sleigh. Taylor galloped after him, but the sleigh didn't slow down as it dashed down the hill. It continued across the frozen river to the opposite side, where two men waited."

"More smugglers?" asked Edouard.

Gerry smiled and held up his finger again. "The sleigh stopped and Taylor galloped his horse across the river, and then shoved his revolver muzzle into the man's face. And the man threw his hands up."

Gerry raised his hands into the air.

"What happened to the men waiting on the shore?" Edouard asked.

"They galloped away," Gerry replied. "Taylor grabbed a revolver from the man's belt. Then Miller's men seized the driver and tied him up."

"Lamoureaux?" Moïse asked.

"Old Lamoureaux," replied Gerry. "And then the driver of the other sleigh, the man that he'd disarmed up the road, drove up."

"Who was it?" Edouard asked, his eyes wide.

"Turns out it was old Wright!" said Gerry.

"No!" said Moïse, laughing. "The police were involved too!"

❦CHAPTER 21

There was a rumble in the distance that grew louder and louder. I stepped out of the house, carrying Alexandre on my hip. Emory ran out of the house after me, while Edouard and Philomène raced out of the barn to where I was standing.

"There it is!" said Edouard.

He pointed at a fancy mahogany-coloured Concord stagecoach as it came into sight. It jolted and swayed and was drawn by six horses that seemed wild and out of control. The horses were driven by Max, another French Canadian who'd moved north with us from Oregon. He wore a six-shooter strapped to his waist and pulled back on the reins when he neared the barn.

"Whoa!" he called out.

The horses trotted their way towards the barn and stopped, and then danced on the spot while the stagecoach's brakes were applied.

Max drove the route between Fort Macleod to Pincher Creek three times every week, carrying the mail and passengers in each direction and changing out horses at our ranch. It was a dangerous job. There was never a mention of the stagecoach being held up on its travels, but Max sometimes told tales of runaway horses, when the reins of the coach were pulled from his grasp and strewn along the trail, along with his passengers' clothing. He also told stories of fording swollen streams and ending up being thrown into the water, away from the stagecoach and his horses.

Max climbed down from his seat, and held his hand out to me. "Hello, Julia!"

"Hello, Max!" I replied.

Edouard bounded up to the stagecoach driver.

"Can I help with the horses?" he asked, enthusiastically. "Do you have any mail today, sir?"

"Hello, Edouard!" said Max, smiling as he ruffled Edouard's hair. "Of course! But first, look who I brought? She's travelled from Montréal to see you."

Max walked up to the stagecoach door and opened it, and took the hand of the young woman inside, helping her descend the steps.

Edouard stared at the woman in front of him and frowned. He wasn't sure what to say.

"I'm pleased to meet you. I'm Emma St. Dénis." The young woman extended her hand towards him and smiled. "I'm your cousin Philomène's daughter."

Edouard frowned. "I have a sister named Philomène."

"She was probably named after my mother," Emma replied. "Your father's sister."

Edouard tentatively took the woman's hand, and then quickly backed away.

I walked over and extended my hand. "Hello, Emma. I'm pleased to meet you."

Emma was moving west to work in the village of Pincher Creek as a seamstress. About one year earlier, Moïse had received a letter from his sister Philomène in Montréal, asking if Emma could come out to stay with us. And over the course of the year, the plans became firmer. She would stay with us until she moved into the village.

Smiling, Emma shook my hand. "Hello, Julia."

"You must be exhausted after your trip," I said. "This is Philomène and Emory."

I smiled down at the little boy I was carrying on my hip. "And this is Alexandre. Come, we'll take you inside."

Emma walked with me to the house, with the smaller children in tow.

"Julia!" Max called after me. "I have a letter for you!"

He waved a letter in the air, and gave it to Edouard, who ran it over to me. I looked at the envelope, and then slipped it into the pocket of my skirt.

"When's your baby due?" Emma asked, as we continued walking towards the house.

I was heavily pregnant again and due in mid-November.

"Next month," I replied. "Although, with the way that I feel now, it could be any day."

"He was a greenhorn!" Moïse told us that night after supper.

Max had joined us, and he and Moïse were amusing everyone with their stories.

"But how could you tell?" Edouard asked.

"He should have been heading for shelter," Moïse replied, matter-of-factly. "But instead, he was driving his team directly into a storm."

"Why would he do that?" Edouard asked.

"A few days earlier, a Chinook had arrived," Moïse continued. "That's probably when he set out."

"What's a Chinook?" asked Emma.

"Warm west winds that sweep down from the mountains," Moïse replied.

"Have you heard the Peigans' legend?" I asked Edouard.

He shook his head.

"There once was a beautiful maiden named Chinook," I began. "She wandered into the foothills and became lost in the mountains. The bravest warriors searched for her, but she was never found again."

"That's so sad," said Philomène.

I nodded. "One day, a warm breeze came over the mountain and melted the snow and ice, just like in Papa's story. The warriors gazed at each other and decided that it was Chinook's breath."

Emma smiled. Then Moïse continued his story about the greenhorn.

"The warm winds blew the snow off the face of the hills, depositing it along the treeline of the creeks and in the gullies, and there were large pools of water that had accumulated in the fields, since the ground was still frozen. But the weather was changing."

"How did you know?" Edouard asked.

"I could see it," Moïse answered. "The Chinook arch had disappeared and the wind had shifted to the north. It became more biting. A storm was coming."

He paused and took a sip of his coffee.

"I'd spent the day riding the range and didn't want to be caught out in the storm. I was riding for home when I saw the greenhorn driving his four-horse team directly into the storm."

"What did you do?" Philomène asked.

"I had to set out after him, but I didn't reach him in time. The storm swallowed up the team."

"Was he killed?" Edouard asked.

Moïse shook his head. "No, but he was very lucky. The snow was so thick that he couldn't tell which direction he was traveling, and he drove directly over the cut bank along the Pincher Creek."

"No!" Max gasped.

Moïse nodded. "Big Swan saw him too and set out after him. He and some other band members arrived at the top of the cut bank. They found the wagon split apart, the horses tangled up in their harnesses and each other, and the contents of the wagon spilled all over the ground."

"What happened to the driver?" Edouard asked.

"He was thrown into a deep snowdrift," Moïse replied. "Big Swan and his men untangled the horses and led them and the driver back to their lodge. And that's where I found him."

"Who was the greenhorn?" Max asked.

"Alexis' son."

After the children were in bed for the night, and the house was quiet, I took the letter out of my pocket and handed it to Moïse.

"Could you please read this to me," I asked.

"Of course."

He took the letter from me, carefully opening the envelope and pulling out the letter. I watched his face as he read it. He frowned, and then I saw his mouth twitch.

"What is it?" I asked.

He looked at me, led me to a nearby chair, and then knelt before me. There were tears in his eyes, as he cleared his throat.

"It's from your Papa."

"Is he okay?" I asked, anxiously.

He nodded.

"What is it?" I asked.

"Victoria has passed away."

"I knew that I shouldn't have left her," I cried, once it had sunk in. I stood up and walked to the window, trying to catch my breath.

Moïse walked over to me and wrapped his arms around me, and I sobbed onto his shoulder.

Oh, Victoria.

Victorine was born in mid-November, named in honour of Victoria. It was a very difficult time. I found myself so busy that I couldn't properly mourn Victoria's death. And yet in retrospect, this was perhaps best. Emma helped with the other children and prepared the meals. The timing of her visit was a godsend. *What will become of Victoria's daughters?*

CHAPTER 22

SPRING 1887

After moving to the North-West Territories, Moïse and every other rancher in the district adopted a very hands-off approach to raising stock. The cattle were fattened on the open range. With no fences, the cattle were turned loose to graze on the rich grasses, and then rounded up only for branding or sale. To be successful in the early days, a rancher needed far more capital than labour. However, this would soon change.

The summer of 1886 had been dry, and the locals were predicting a mild winter. At first, there appeared to be some merit in this prediction. By November, only a few inches of snow lay on the ground, making it easy for the cattle to forage. Yet by Christmas, the temperature plummeted and wouldn't budge. Then a blizzard blew in, blanketing the plains with over two feet of snow. Initially, the local ranchers weren't overly concerned.

"We've seen this before," they said. "A Chinook's just around the corner."

After all, the presence of the warm Chinook winds to break up the frigid winter cold was the very reason why most of the ranchers had moved to this corner of the country. Yet by February, there was still no relief, and cattle began to die on the range.

Moïse stood at the frosted window, looking out at the slopes, which were normally swept clear of snow by the strong prevailing west wind.

"They're covered!" he growled. "That's why we moved to this property."

Then the Chinook arches began appearing, warming the frigid air and melting the top layer of snow. Yet they were short-lived, snuffed out by another blast of Arctic air, leaving in their wake a hard crust on the snow.

"They're too weak to paw through it!" Moïse barked, stomping his foot onto the ground. He'd just returned from riding the range to check on the cattle.

"Can you buy hay?" I asked as I returned from the milk house, which I'd just finished scouring with boiling water.

"There's no hay to buy. And now, the cattle are drifting and milling in the coulees, where they're freezing to death."

The conditions worsened with each passing day, dumping snow over the frozen bodies of the dead cows until mid-March, when the weather finally broke. The temperature rose so quickly that the ice on the Oldman River broke up, flooding the low-lying land from the village of Pincher Creek eastward towards Kipp. The floodwaters melted the remaining snow and exposed hundreds of carcasses.

The ranchers in the district were hit hard, most of them losing between a quarter and half of their livestock. And as the temperatures rose, the air was filled with the rank smell of rotting flesh. Diphtheria ravaged the district.

The disease swept through our family. Edouard, Philomène, and Emory were the first family members stricken with the disease. Their symptoms were relatively mild, and all the children fought valiantly. However, the disease seemed to strengthen as it moved on to the younger children. Two-year-old Alexandre and four-month old Victorine battled against "the strangler."

"We need the doctor," I told Moïse as I watched both children struggling for breath and burning up with fever.

They'd both taken a turn for the worse, and their condition seemed to be deteriorating rapidly. Moïse galloped his horse to Fort Macleod, but it was too late.

First, Victorine passed away in my arms. The tiny girl swaddled in a light blanket looked into my eyes as she struggled for breath, and then closed her eyes and became silent.

Struggling to control my grief, I laid her little body into her bassinet, and then went to tend little Alexandre. His small cheeks were flushed, and he gasped for air. I dabbed a cool cloth on his forehead and tenderly pushed locks of fine black hair away from his brow. I then leaned forward and gently kissed his cheek. *Please, don't take him too.*

I stroked his brow and began to sing to him.

> "*Fais dodo, mon petit Pierrot,*
> *J' t'apprendrai à filer la laine,*
> *Fais dodo, mon petit Pierrot,*
> *J' t'apprendrai à fair' des sabots.*"

His breathing quieted. He was no longer suffering. I became overcome with grief, and sobs wracked my body.

I knelt by two freshly covered mounds, completely overcome with grief. There was a small wooden cross at the head of each mound, on the top of a hill where the water would never reach. Moïse slowly made his way over to me, holding the hands of Philomène and Emory, and was followed closely by Edouard. When they reached me, I stood up. Moïse let go of the children's hands, and then put his arms around me. I turned and sobbed onto his shoulder, my entire body shaking with grief. The three children stood side-by-side, motionless. They were anxious and unsure what they should do or how they should act. It scared them to see me cry. Moïse said a few words over the tiny graves, and then we all turned slowly and walked away.

CHAPTER 23

SUMMER 1887

Life changed for the ranchers around the district. No longer would they rely on the open range to sustain their livestock over the long winter months. Instead, beginning in mid-July, the staccato rhythm of the horse-drawn mower was heard at the ranches as the haying operation began. The ranchers also began contracting out the haying work.

On the first weekend in August, once the hay had been cut, dried, and put up into the hayloft, a horse race was held at our homestead. Everyone from the district attended the races, including the French Canadian group, the English contingent, the Scottish element, and the Peigans. And each group brought their best racehorses. There were names like Frenchie, Oceoleo, Rooster, Apple Jack, Gold Dust, and Beauty.

There were races over different distances and for different purses, presided over by a panel of judges that ruled the races and started each one with the firing of a pistol. Moïse's colt Fortier ran his first race and placed second in the 5/8-mile dash, winning a prize of $15. Moïse was immensely proud.

"He's a fine horse," Moïse told me of his beloved Fortier. "He'll be a great horse one day."

The races were followed by a ball. That day, the sound of the music drifted out of our barn and into the valley, bouncing off the steep walls of the deep gorge of Pincher Creek, upstream from where it spilled into the Oldman River.

Edouard walked out of the barn carrying his fiddle in one hand and his bow in the other. He sat down beside me on a chair outside the barn. His cheeks were flushed, and his dark brown hair was slicked back off his brow. He inhaled the blissful scent of the freshly cut hay that seemed to fill the air.

A few more people spilled out of the barn.

"You play well!" said one man, thumping Edouard's thin shoulders as he walked past.

"Almost as well as your papa!" another man added, chuckling.

Moïse emerged from the barn's interior holding a fiddle under his arm and a bow in his hand. He held himself proudly as he walked over to Edouard.

"Very good!" he declared, putting his hand Edouard's shoulder.

"Thank you, Papa," said Edouard, beaming at his father.

At fifteen, he was the same height as Moïse, but had a finer build.

Remi soon joined them. He carried a comb covered with a piece of paper and also inhaled the fresh air deeply.

"Hello," he said, bowing slightly to me, smiling with a twinkle in his eyes. "How are you doing?"

"It helps to be busy," I told him, smiling politely, and then looked toward the hill where the two little children were buried.

Moïse squeezed my shoulder lightly, and then turned to face Remi.

"Did you see LeBoeuf's horse?"

Remi laughed. "Threw his rider three times!"

Moïse laughed too. "But is he ever talented," he said, smoothing the hairs of his large moustache.

Remi nodded. "And Scott's Rooster," he added, whistling.

Moïse looked over at the hay fields, which were now devoid of hay, his expression becoming serious. He looked back at Remi.

"Would you ever go back?"

"Where?" Remi asked, frowning. "Québec?"

Moïse shook his head.

"Oregon."

Remi shook his head.

"Grazing's better here," he said, a twinkle appearing in his eyes as he slapped Moïse on the shoulder. "Plus, my friends are here."

Moïse smiled, and then continued.

"It's been a tough year."

Remi nodded. "Time heals," he said, patting his friend on the back. "Life's better here. I saw Max. He said the rail line's moving this way."

"The train!" Edouard exclaimed.

His eyes were wide. He'd seen a train—the Oregon Pacific Railroad—before we immigrated to Canada. He'd heard the sound of the distant steam whistle heralding the train's arrival and had been mesmerized by the sight of it, watching the connecting rods on the wheels, moving ever faster as the train's speed increased, and the large plume of smoke escaping from the locomotive's chimney. He longed to travel on one. In fact, he longed to travel.

Remi nodded.

"They won't need the stagecoach," said Moïse.

"Why?" Edouard asked.

"The train'll carry the mail and the passengers," Moïse explained. "They won't need to cross through the Oldman here. People won't stop here anymore."

"But it'll open up markets for us," Remi added. "For our livestock."

"But there's too many farmers wanting to move in," said Moïse, shaking his head. "The ranchers will lose out."

"*C'est la vie,*" Remi replied.

"*Oui, c'est la vie,*" agreed Moïse

He looked tired as he turned to me. "Will you be okay?" he asked, softly.

I nodded.

Moïse turned to Remi and Edouard. "Let's play more music before we eat!"

"Yes, let's," Remi replied, placing his arm around Edouard's shoulders, before the trio strode back into the barn.

CHAPTER 24

SPRING 1888

Emma was born that spring. We named her after Moïse's niece, and I had so many mixed feelings about her birth. Although I was thrilled to be blessed with another baby, and another daughter, after having Alexandre and baby Victorine snatched from me, I was scared to death of death itself. Any little cough or tummy upset in one of the children had me on edge. As a result, I tried to keep them in the fresh air as much as possible and would often take them with me to the creek.

I loved this location on Pincher Creek. The valley dramatically narrowed into a steep, deep gorge covered in native evergreens, with an outcrop of sandstone-coloured rock on the west side. After the spring rains, the normally dormant landscape would become painted in vivid colours. Lush green grass was interspersed with delicate yellow, pink, and purple wildflowers, and the Saskatoons covering the side of the hills looked like a sea of white, fluffy round blossoms, framed by the rugged mountains to the west.

I'd wash the laundry in the creek as Emma slept beside me in her cradleboard, while the older children played on the hill or swam in the swimming hole at the bend of the creek. At the age of fifteen, Edouard had told me that he was too old for these activities, but on a hot, still day, he'd be the first of the kids to jump into the cool, refreshing water. The sound of their squeals and laughter filled me with joy.

"Mama?" Philomène said to me, one hot afternoon in July as she climbed out of the creek.

"Mmm," I replied, absently lifting a skirt out of the water.

"Why do people call you a half-breed?" she asked, wrapping a towel around her shoulders and climbing onto a rock beside me.

"Who called me that?" I asked, twisting the skirt to squeeze out the water.

"The people yesterday," she replied, looking up at me with a serious expression on her face.

She pulled the towel more tightly around her shoulders. She resembled Victoria more and more, and on some days, I found myself catching my breath as I caught glimpses of my sister.

"The ones that crossed the river," said Philomène.

I shook the skirt, trying to remove some of the wrinkles.

"Some people aren't kind," I replied. "And others don't know any better."

"Lots of people say that," Edouard added, scowling and sitting down on a rock.

I looked up at him, and he nodded with a look of defiance.

"What does it mean, though?" asked Philomène.

"They're referring to the fact that I'm part Sioux, and part French Canadian," I explained.

"Why does that make you a half-breed?" she said, looking puzzled.

I shrugged. "It doesn't. It's just a rude saying."

"So, we're half-breeds too?" she asked.

"I guess, if you want to call us that," I replied, nodding. "But this isn't a kind thing to say."

"Then why do they say this?" she asked.

"Because we're different from them," I replied.

I spread the skirt out on a rock, and then sat down and looked at her.

"Is that bad?" she asked.

"No, of course not," I replied, rubbing my hand over her towel-covered arm. "But sometimes when people are afraid, they react this way. They're different from us too."

"I hate them!" Edouard snapped.

"No," I said, shooting a glance at him. "Then you're no better than they are."

He looked embarrassed.

"Don't let anyone make you feel bad for who you are," I continued. "Or where you came from."

"Are you proud?" Philomène asked.

I nodded and smiled. "But it doesn't mean that I have to volunteer information to everyone."

She frowned. "What do you mean?"

"It doesn't make me any less proud by being careful who I share this information with."

Philomène nodded.

I looked upstream at a bird that was circling overhead, gliding on the air currents. I often thought about the world that my children were growing up in. It was changing. New people were moving in every day, many from areas of the world that were foreign to me. I wasn't sure how accepting of us they would be if they knew where I came from.

"What do you tell your children about your past?" I asked Martha the next day, when she and Remi and their daughters stopped by for supper.

We'd finished our supper and the men had wandered outside to look at the horses, while the children were outside playing in the yard.

"I've told them everything," she said, drying the plate that I'd handed to her. "They know where I come from."

"Do they ever tell anyone?" I asked, rubbing a dishcloth over another plate.

She shook her head.

"Only family and close friends. It won't do them any good if too many people know."

"Is that okay?" I asked, frowning.

"What do you mean?" she said, as we both sat down at the table.

"Won't they forget who they are?"

She shook her head. "I won't let them."

"But won't they end up ashamed of who they are?"

"No," she replied, shaking her head again. "It isn't acceptable being a half-breed. And you're considered a half-breed with only a drop of Indian blood. We'll celebrate this within the family, but they mustn't repeat it outside the circle."

Toward the end of summer, the wild berries were abundant in the creek and river bottoms, and we invited the families in the district to come over and pick them. All of the families brought baskets of food, and at lunchtime, we stopped picking berries to eat a picnic lunch of chicken, sandwiches, salads, and tasty desserts. In the afternoon, the men disappeared in the direction of the barn and the livestock, the children ran toward the hills to play tag and games of hide and seek, while the women scoured the shrubs on the hills near the creek for berries.

"They're called candied violets," Martha told us as we picked Saskatoons halfway down the side of the hill. "And they're considered a delicacy."

She popped a few Saskatoons into her mouth.

"Mmm. These are so sweet!" she said, closing her eyes to emphasize her point. "They're going to make the best syrup!"

"Yes, they will, but tell me more about candied violets," said Flora, a neighbour who lived on a homestead northwest of ours.

Martha nodded. "They're also called preserved violets."

I smiled. Martha had become a dear friend, but she could be so dramatic at times. She also loved to be the centre of attention when she was telling us a story.

"They sold them in Montréal too," Moïse's niece, Emma, added.

She was now engaged to be married to one of the men in town. The wedding would be held that fall.

"But how on earth would you prepare them?" Flora asked.

"You boil sugar in water, and then add the violets," explained Martha. "But only a few at a time."

She stopped picking the berries, dipped her hand into her basket, and began eating.

"And don't remove them until the water has boiled again and the sugar turns white. And then you coat the flowers and let them drain on a cloth."

"Do you eat them for dessert?" I asked, remembering a patch of violets growing at the base of some of the trees near the house.

She nodded.

"Have you tried them?" Flora asked Martha.

Martha shook her head.

"I read this in the paper."

"Chewing violets freshens your breath," Emma added. "Some of the ladies in New York are doing that."

I spotted some shrubs near the water that were laden with dark purple, plump Saskatoons that bent the branches downward with their weight. I wandered over to the shrubs, instinctively glancing down at the muddy shore, just as I'd once done with Grandmother many years earlier, scanning the area for tracks.

Then I spotted something. There were five distinct toe imprints, wide and shaped like a triangle. My eyes widened. I noticed more.

The tracks led away from the river's edge, upstream from where I stood. I bent down and examined the prints more closely. Above each toe was a small dot pushed into the sand, evidence of a sharp nail.

Bear tracks!

A gust of wind blew from behind me, carrying my scent upstream towards the brush. I panicked and looked up at the brush, scanning the area. And there it was, forty or fifty feet away. It reared up onto its hind legs.

I didn't move, paralyzed with fear. Then the wind gusted from behind me again, catching my skirt and billowing it out, doubling my width, and then flapping it like a sail. The bear continued to stare at me, turning sideways. The wind also carried the women's voices and laughter, along with the sounds of the children laughing and screaming on the hill. Little Emma, who'd been asleep in the cradleboard strapped to my back, had awakened and was gurgling and cooing happily.

The bear snapped its jaws a few times, and then lowered itself onto all fours and lumbered off upstream away from me. I quickly turned and scrambled up the hill toward the other women. They stopped talking and stared at me.

"What is it?" Martha asked, rushing forward. "What happened?"

I pointed upstream near the creek. "Bear!"

"Children!" Martha shouted up the hill to where the children were playing. "Run back to the house as fast as you can!"

We picked up the baskets and hurried after them, heading for the safety of the house.

"It was big and black," I told Moïse as I pulled the cradleboard off my back and rested it against a chair in the kitchen.

I was greeted by a large smile from Emma, who was still securely strapped to the cradleboard. I looked out the window, scanning the yard for the older children and breathing a huge sigh of relief once I spotted them playing with the others.

"Black bear," he replied.

"They don't normally travel down out of the mountains this far," added Gerry.

"Probably followed the creek down," Remi suggested.

"And was attracted to the berries," Moïse nodded. "It's a bumper crop, after all."

I took a seat beside Emma. Although the encounter had probably lasted only a few minutes at the most, I felt drained and immensely relieved.

"Have you had any wolves?" Remi asked.

Moïse nodded. "They've killed calves and foals," he said. "They even got my bell mare!"

A few weeks earlier, when I'd been walking back to the house at dawn, after finishing my morning chores, I'd seen the mule lying on the ground in her field. I'd run over to her but found her in a horrible, bloody state. And there had been nothing that I could do.

"They killed her!" Moïse growled.

Remi nodded.

"They're cruel animals—eat their prey alive."

"A Stoney man caught ten on our property," said Moïse. "He got a ten-dollar bounty on their heads, and he earned every dollar of it."

Remi whistled.

We had a small herd of dairy cows on the homestead that I tended to each day. Each morning, I walked out to the cow paddock and buckled a halter onto the angular-shaped head of one of the cows. I led her into the barn and secured stanchions around her head to lock it in place, before placing a bucket of feed in front of her.

Immediately, she'd put her face into the bucket and begin chewing a mouthful of pellets, and turn to look at me. I loved these cows, with their pink rounded noses, large brown eyes, and expressive ears. She'd put her nose back into the bucket to grab another mouthful. In Oregon, Moïse had taught me the entire milking process, from cleaning the cow's udder to testing the milk and sterilizing the bottles.

Once the cow was milked, I'd clean her udder, release her from the stanchions, and lead her back to the paddock, and then halter the next cow and begin the process again. I enjoyed my time alone with the cows, although some mornings, Edouard woke up early and helped me. I always enjoyed this time with him too.

"I want to help with the round-up," he told me one morning that fall.

"You're too young," I said, gently.

"Papa says that I'm a good enough rider," he countered.

I shook my head. I wished that Moïse would speak to me first before putting ideas into Edouard's head that I had to squash.

"You're a very good rider. It's just that I think that you're too young."

"But the other boys my age will be helping."

I looked up at him. His eyes were almost dancing.

"Papa will be there," he pleaded. "I'd be careful."

"Let me speak to your father about it."

Once all of the cows were milked, I'd carry the milk to a shed, where I separated it and made butter. This was my domain, and I didn't allow anyone else to step foot into the building but me. I kept the shed meticulously clean, wearing a scarf over my hair before entering and always donning a clean apron as I scalded every surface of the shed with boiling water.

Naturally, because the children weren't allowed into the milk shed, this became the one location on the homestead where they loved to play. They'd play in circles around the building, daring each other to go near or even set foot in the shed. As soon as I saw this taking place, I'd shoo them away.

One day, I walked to the milk shed carrying a large pot of boiling water. I saw Emory standing near the entrance to the shed, smiling broadly at me.

"Scoot!" I called to him. "You know that you aren't allowed in here. How many times do I have to remind you? No one's allowed in my milk shed but me. Now go!"

He laughed and sped off towards the barn. I began scalding the surfaces within the milk shed, humming softly to myself as I worked. Every now and then, I winced as the boiling water made contact with my hands or arms. Once the pot was empty, I walked into the fresh air and wiped the perspiration from my nose and brow with my sleeve. I stood for a moment, allowing the slight breeze to wrap its cool arms around me, breathing in its freshness, before walking over to the pump to fill the pot full of water.

I heard a loud bang from the direction of the barn, followed by the thunderous, rhythmic sound of a horse galloping. Then silence. I let go of the pump handle, dropped the pot, and ran toward the barn, holding up my skirt up so that I wouldn't trip on it.

When I reached the barn, Edouard and Philomène were kneeling next to Emory, who lay crumpled on the ground just inside the barn door. I ran inside and picked the little boy up. His body was limp.

"What happened?" I asked.

"He jumped onto one of the horses," Edouard cried. "I tried to stop him, but he wouldn't listen."

"And the horse spooked," Philomène added. "It bolted out the barn door."

Edouard nodded. "He didn't duck his head as the horse galloped out the door. He hit his head on the frame and fell off."

"Get your father," I told Edouard. "Tell him to get Dr. Kennedy!" I ran towards the house with Emory in my arms and placed him on his bed. A short time later, he regained consciousness and complained of a terrible headache. Dr. Kennedy rode up with Moïse several hours later and examined Emory.

"He's suffered a concussion," Dr. Kennedy explained. "You'll have to keep him quiet. And don't let him sleep for more than one hour at a time for a few days."

"Will he recover?" I asked.

"He should," replied Dr. Kennedy, nodding. "He's a very lucky boy."

Nevertheless, Emory's fearlessness continued. I tried to keep him away from the horses, but the precocious six-year-old always gravitated to them.

"Don't fight it," Moïse warned me.

"I don't want him to get hurt," I snapped.

"Then we'll teach him properly," said Moïse.

So Moïse began to teach Emory how to ride and handle horses. He began on Poppy and progressed to one of Moïse's trusted old horses. Edouard and Moïse also wore me down with their constant lecturing, insisting that Edouard was old enough to accompany Moïse at the round-up.

"They had a rodeo afterwards," Edouard told me, after he returned from the round-up.

I looked at him, but didn't say a word.

"The cowboys rode bucking horses," he added. "Sometimes without saddles, sometimes with them."

"Did they get bucked off?" Emory asked, excitedly.

"Sometimes," replied Edouard. "But some of the riders were so good. It looked like the horses were only rocking instead of trying to buck them off their backs. I'm going to do that next year."

He ran out of the house toward the barn.

"Me too!" Emory declared, running after him.

I looked over at Moïse and frowned. He chuckled and smiled back at me.

CHAPTER 25

My son Pierre was born during a torrential rainstorm that lasted all day and overnight turned to a blizzard driven by a bitter north wind. Although it was already May, winter seemed reluctant to relinquish its hold.

"The snow'll be short-lived," Moïse told me, as I rocked a sleeping Pierre in my arms and stared bleakly at the white land-scape beyond the window.

Spring marked the start of mass immigration into North America. Many of the new immigrants were moving from the eastern region of Europe, which was in the midst of a cholera out-break that had killed thousands of people.

"Eighty deaths a day," said Moïse, whistling.

"Where?" I asked, looking up from the loaf of bread that I'd just taken out of the oven.

"St. Petersburg," replied Moïse, reading aloud from the news-paper that was open on the kitchen table. "In Russia."

"Oh, those poor people," I murmured, setting the loaf pan beside four others on a cooling rack. "Will it spread here?"

Moïse shrugged his shoulders.

"It's hard to say."

The disease spread throughout Europe, reaching epidemic proportions. There was growing fear in the US that it would enter that country too.

"Ships docking in American ports have sick people on board," Martha told me, when she and Remi had stopped in on their way to Fort Macleod for supplies.

"Ships from Europe?" I asked.

She nodded. "But the US government is quarantining the passengers on board."

"That's wise," I replied.

"Hamburg's had over fourteen thousand cases," said Martha.

I looked up from the sock that I was darning. "Fourteen thousand!" I gasped

She nodded. "And nine thousand deaths!"

By September, the number of infected immigrants arriving at American ports was increasing.

"New York State bought a hotel on a place called Fire Island," Moïse read aloud to me from the newspaper. "To hold quarantined immigrants."

"Is the Dominion government doing anything?" I asked.

"They're fumigating quarantined steamers in Québec," Moïse explained.

I handed him a cup of coffee and sat down beside him at the kitchen table. "Will that stop the disease?"

Moïse shrugged. "They're fumigating passengers and baggage before they journey farther west."

"Journey farther west?" I echoed. "They're allowing them to move out here?"

Moïse sighed and nodded. "They're holding infected vessels at Grosse Island for ten days. And if there's cholera on board, they're quarantined for twenty days, then thoroughly disinfected."

I shuddered.

Around that time, the Canadian Pacific Railway announced its intentions to build a line from Fort Macleod through the Crow's Nest Pass into British Columbia's West Kootenay region. Following this news, there was a flurry of activity around Fort Macleod, as the railroad company's engineers arrived in order to determine the best route through the area.

"We need to purchase some of your land," one of the Canadian Pacific Railway engineers told Moïse as we stood on the top of the cut bank above the creek.

"Do you?" said Moïse, raising his eyebrows and stroking his large moustache.

"Yes, we're building the line across your property," the man replied.

"Across my property," said Moïse.

"Yes," the man added. "And a bridge will cross the creek here."

"A bridge?" I asked, frowning.

The creek was my favourite part of the homestead. I didn't want to lose a piece of it for a train to travel through.

"Yes, ma'am," the man replied.

"How big is the bridge?" Moïse asked.

"A twelve-hundred-foot timber trestle," the man replied, proudly.

"Why so long?" asked Moïse.

The man pointed down the hill to the creek, then up the hill on the west side of the water. "The cut bank is steep here."

"How tall?' Moïse asked.

"One hundred and ten feet."

Moïse was still incensed when Remi and Martha joined us for supper a few days later.

"Can you believe the size?" he said, thumping the table with his hand.

Remi shook his head slightly.

"Yeah. They'd need to keep the tracks over the water at the same height as at the top of the cutback."

"Yes," Moïse added. "But why here? Why couldn't it be farther south?"

Remi shrugged.

"They had surveyors out. They must've decided that it was the best line."

"What if I refuse to sell to them?" Moïse asked, crossing his arms over his chest.

"I don't think that you can," Remi replied, quietly.

Remi turned out to be correct, and an agreement was drawn up to sell the railroad company twelve acres of our land.

Over the next few years, the cholera epidemic in Europe worsened. The North Atlantic Steamship Confederation instructed all European agents to refuse bookings from any German emigrants bound for the US or Canada, unless the person had been out of Germany for at least three weeks prior to the shipping date.

"Canada's only allowing in British and Scandinavian immigrants," Moïse read from the newspaper.

Although these restrictions slowed the spread of the disease within Canada, by the summer of 1894, cases were being reported.

"Two hundred deaths in Montréal in June," Moïse read from the newspaper.

"They still haven't stopped the spread?" I asked.

Moïse shook his head. "It seems to be worse where conditions are crowded," Moïse replied, pausing before he read more. "There's cases of typhoid fever too."

"There was a case of typhoid fever here," I remarked, trying to recall the details. "A few years back, I think?"

Moïse looked up at me and nodded. "In Pincher Creek, at the North-West Mounted Police."

"And the man died," I added.

Moïse continued reading. "It says that some cities flush out their sewers onto the frozen creeks."

I grimaced. "Why?"

He shook his head. "Ranchers dispose of livestock carcasses on the frozen rivers too."

"And then people drink the water?" I asked.

Moïse nodded and looked up at me. "It says people should boil or filter the water."

Emma started school that fall. She was our first child to attend and boarded at the school in Pincher Creek during the week. Moïse would drop her off after church on Sundays, and then pick her up and bring her home on Fridays. Although it was early to be dropped off for school, we'd decided that this was the best arrangement, given our distance from the school. And there were other children who were dropped off at the same time. The nuns looked after them and fed them their supper. Despite the large French Canadian contingent in the district, everything was taught in English, which Emma didn't know when she began attending.

"The nuns won't let us speak French," she complained to me, after her first week.

I held her in my arms and rocked her gently.

"Not even when we eat our meals," she said, with tears in her eyes. "They even hit my hand with a ruler when I forgot and spoke to Marie in French."

She held out her tiny hand for me to see. I could still make out the outline of the ruler on her hand.

"They hit her!" I told Moïse later that night, once the children were asleep.

"Who did?" he asked, frowning.

"One of the nuns!"

I was incensed. I didn't believe in hitting children.

"Oh," Moïse replied, returning his attention back to newspapers in front of him.

"That's all you have to say?" I asked, frowning at him.

"It was a nun," he said. "When I went to school, the nuns would hit us if we were bad."

"But she was hit for speaking French!" I exclaimed.

Moïse merely shrugged. "She'll learn."

Soon after this, the French Canadian families formed an organization that arranged sports days, picnics, horse races, dances, and outings on Beauvais Lake. At one of the dances, Edouard met a girl named Célina, the daughter of one of the local families in the district.

"I'll drop you off at her house, on the way to church," Moïse told Edouard, who'd been invited to Célina's for Sunday lunch.

I stood out on the porch and waved to Emma, who sat in the back of the wagon. It still pained me greatly to see her leave for school each week. She also wasn't eating properly. She'd dropped weight since starting the school year.

I waved until the wagon was out of sight, and then pulled my sweater around me. I turned to walk back into the house when movement in the brush west of the house caught my attention. I scanned the area, hoping to identify whatever it was. Then I saw a man crouching.

"*Mon Dieu!*" I exclaimed.

I raced into the house and slammed the door behind me.

CHAPTER 26

"Quick," I called to the children. "Hide in the closet."

"What is it?" Philomène asked as I ran up the stairs and ushered Emory and Pierre into the closet in the front bedroom. Then she looked out the window and screamed.

"Please keep them quiet," I said, holding a finger to my lips.

"There's a man," she cried, the colour draining from her face. "He has a gun."

"Into the closet," I said, staring at her. "Please."

No sooner had I pulled the closet door closed than the front door suddenly burst open. I stifled a shriek with my hand.

There was the sound of shuffling in the kitchen. We then heard the sound of footsteps heading out of the house and onto the gravel outside. I opened the closet door and peeked out. All was quiet in the house.

"Stay put," I said, as I looked back at the children and held a finger to my lips.

I darted to the bedroom window and looked out, watching the man disappear into the brush.

"Stay here," I whispered to the children.

I crept out to the kitchen, where I immediately noticed that the front door was ajar. I closed it, then looked around the kitchen. The loaves of bread that I'd baked that morning were gone, as was the roast that I'd cooked and prepared for our dinner, but nothing else seemed to be missing.

"Everything's fine," I called to the children.

Within the hour, two policemen rode up to the house.

"Can I help you?" I asked, still feeling somewhat shaken from the earlier events.

"We're looking for a Blood Indian," one of them told me.

I relayed the story to them of the break-in that had just occurred.

"It's gotta be him," said the other policemen.

"What did he do?" I asked

"He killed a sergeant," the man replied, spitting onto the ground. "And made other attempts at murder."

I frowned.

"But he saw me, when he was still outside," I frowned. "He must have known that the children were here."

"He's dangerous," the first man told me. "We need reinforcements. We already sent a messenger to Pincher Creek asking for back-up."

Moïse was upset when he got home. "He must have watched us leave," he said, pounding his hand on the kitchen table.

"But he knew that I was here," I added. "And he didn't harm me or the children."

"But he could have!" roared Moïse, scowling.

"Yes," I said "But he didn't. He only took food."

"You and the kids have to stay close until he's caught!" Moïse insisted.

The police eventually found the man. When he was captured, he politely asked them to return a knife to me, which he'd taken when he grabbed the loaves of bread. I was touched by this gesture.

"Why would he return it?" asked Edouard.

"Because I believe that, deep down, he's a good man," I replied, as Moïse frowned. I ignored him. "Sometimes, people are driven to doing things that they don't mean to."

And that wasn't the only time that we had encounters with fugitives. Later that year, there was a massive manhunt that stretched from northwest of Calgary to the Kootenays, and to the Oldman District. One day, after Moïse left for Fort Macleod for supplies, the children and I were sitting down for lunch when a man burst into the house, wielding a large knife.

He said something to me, but I shook my head. I didn't understand what he was saying. He repeated his words in Blackfoot: "I'm hungry."

I nodded, and replied that we were just about to eat. The man took a seat with the knife on the table beside him. I brought the food to the table, and he began wolfing it down.

"Where are you from?" he asked.

"Iowa."

"You're Blackfoot?" he asked.

I shook my head. "Sioux, but I was raised by the Blackfoot."

"I didn't do it," he told me, as if my believing in him was important.

"No?" I asked.

"But they're after me."

He left our house following the meal and disappeared. We heard later that he'd been captured by the police and shot.

"Shot?" I said, frowning. "Why?"

"He was a fugitive," Moïse replied.

With the completion of the rail lines from Calgary to Edmonton, and from Calgary to Fort Macleod, ranchers began shipping their cattle eastward. Annual round-ups and cattle drives were held to move the cattle the short distance to the railway.

The farmers new to the district heralded the coming of CPR's Crowsnest railway line. It would open up new markets for their crops. At the time, the farmers were only able to carry eighty bushels of grain, at most, in the back of a wagon. All they could do was grow crops for their own consumption and the small local and well-supplied market.

Moïse stood at the window and watched wagon after wagon cross the river at our homestead, carrying heavy pieces of farm machinery. He shook his head.

"It'll be the death of us ranchers."

"What's it for?" I asked, standing next to him by the window.

"For their farm operations."

"Why do they need equipment that's so big?" I asked.

"They're expecting to ship their crops by railcar once the line's built," he replied, frowning. "They'll take over."

Construction of the Crowsnest line began in the summer, starting at Lethbridge. The two hundred and ninety miles of track would run northwest to Fort Macleod, and then west into the Crowsnest Pass. It required thousands of workers and hundreds of horses to pull the heavy wagons filled with equipment and supplies as the construction progressed.

The workers lived in tent camps along the line, and Edouard took a job helping the cook prepare food for the men.

"Are you sure that you want to prepare food?" I asked him, when he suggested the idea.

Edouard nodded.

"You don't know much about cooking," I reminded him.

"But I'll learn," he told me, adamantly.

Edouard had been on the job for two weeks and returned home for a visit on his day off.

"There was fog inside the tent," he said, laughing as he relayed the story. "The men tripped over one another!"

"Inside the tent?" asked Emory, frowning. "Where'd it come from?"

"Steam from the food," Edouard continued. "And it was so cold that the walls of the tent were solid sheets of ice!"

"That must have been horrible," I said.

He nodded. "And fights break out all the time."

"They do?" I asked.

I didn't like the idea of Edouard working in such a volatile place.

Edouard nodded again. "If the teamsters don't deliver liquor to the camps, fights break out!"

Emory's eyes were wide as he listened.

"It's too dangerous," I warned Edouard. "I don't want you to go back there."

"Ah, Mama!" said Edouard, jumping to his feet.

"It's too dangerous," I told Moïse, later that evening.

"It's a tough group," he agreed. "The company notifies the police in advance of pay day too."

"Why?" I asked.

"Reinforcements for the detachments," Moïse replied. "In town."

There was also a group of men following the camps, scavenging what they could. There was a continuous flow of them trudging to and from the camps, no matter what hour of the day. These men caused all kinds of trouble. The situation became so bad that the police began making weekly visits to each camp, which seemed to have a calming effect.

By December, the paperwork for the CPR's purchase of our twelve acres was completed, and the construction of the bridge over the Pincher Creek began. All of the pieces of the trestle were constructed and numbered in Haneyville, CPR's yard south of Fort Macleod. The pieces were then shipped like a giant jigsaw puzzle and reassembled on site.

But once they'd arrived, the workers had to contend with Mother Nature. The extremely bitter wind blew incessantly, delaying the reassembly work and inflicting frostbite on the many workers who were rushing to complete the bridge assembly ahead of the rail gangs.

Temperatures moderated a great deal in December and stayed mild into January, but the winds didn't let up. The workers proceeded cautiously, reinforcing each piece of deck before moving to the next.

"Look at that!"

I pointed out the window, where powerful headlights lit up the bridge, enabling a shift of workers to continue working through the night hours. The busy scene resembled a small town.

"They're under lots of pressure," said Moïse, joining me at the window. "Their grant from the government is conditional on a timely completion of the project."

By late January, the construction was again hampered by a heavy snowfall and strong winds, but despite this, the bridge was somehow completed by the second of February. The track-laying gang, who had waited for a month at the crossing east of the bridge, then began laying the track across the bridge.

CHAPTER 27

1899

Edouard and Célina were married at St. Michaels Catholic Church in Pincher Creek. After the church service, a lunch and dance were held at the ranch belonging to Célina's family, located southwest of the town. It was a beautiful meal, and the dance started out lively, with Célina's father, Alexis, playing the fiddle for the guests. However, Moïse and I left the dance earlier than planned, as he wasn't feeling well.

"Do you want for us to come home now?" Edouard asked me, as he and Remi helped Moïse into the wagon.

"No," I replied, waving him off, and then smiling at him and kissing his cheek. "You enjoy the celebration."

Edouard turned and walked back into the barn.

"Do you want us to go with you?" Remi asked.

I shook my head. "No, we'll be fine," I said, as I smiled and picked up the reins. "I'll get him home and into bed for a rest."

"We'll drop the kids off later," said Martha, kissing my cheek softly. "After the dance."

"Thank you," I whispered as I hugged her.

When we arrived home, Moïse went straight to bed, complaining of nausea. I prepared a mint tea for him. It seemed to settle his stomach, but he remained in bed for about a week. I found this a little unsettling since he was never ill.

Over the following months, he continued to suffer from bouts of nausea, shortness of breath, and would sometimes arrive back at the house, after completing a daily chore, completely drenched in sweat, despite having cold hands and feet. One day, Dr. Kennedy examined Moïse.

"I'm afraid it's your heart," Dr. Kennedy explained.

I looked from Dr. Kennedy to Moïse, whose skin had a greyish sallowness. A lump formed in my throat, making it difficult to swallow.

"What can we do?" I asked.

"There's not much that we can do," replied Dr. Kennedy, smiling softly at me.

Moïse nodded, and then closed his eyes and rested his head back on the pillow. The following spring, he passed away peacefully in his sleep. I heard him take his last breath. It woke me from my restless slumber, and I knew that he was gone.

He was buried at the cemetery on the outskirts of Pincher Creek and almost every rancher in the district attended his funeral. Everyone had a kind word to say to me that day and made me promise to call on them when I needed help.

And then they were gone, and the children and I stood alone at Moïse's grave.

"I have to plant a tree," I told Edouard.

There wasn't a single tree in the cemetery, and I was afraid that the blowing wind would cause the large white stone at the head of Moïse's grave to crumble over time. Edouard put his arm around me.

"We'll plant one."

"It'll provide him some protection from the wind," I said, my voice quivering. "And some shade during the summer."

He squeezed my arm gently.

"And what does the inscription say?" I asked, looking at the large white stone that was covered with ivy leaves.

Only half of the stone was inscribed. A chill ran through me as I realized that, one day, my name would appear next to Moïse's.

"God's fingers touched him, and he slept," Edouard replied softly.

I nodded and closed my eyes; then we walked back to the wagon and Edouard drove us home.

EPILOGUE

Julia continued to run the stopping house after Moïse's death, along with Edouard, his wife Célina, and their children. In 1904, Julia applied for a homestead at that location. By that time, the home, outbuildings, and other improvements were worth $1,885. Ninety-five acres were in crop, and large herds of cattle, along with horses and pigs, were being raised. Unable to read or write, Julia signed her name with an "X" that was accompanied by a stamp reading, "So Help Me God."

Sometime prior to her death on February 3, 1937, Julia moved from the LaGrandeur Crossing into the Scott Block in Pincher Creek. She was buried next to Moïse in the Roman Catholic Cemetery in Pincher Creek. Her half of the stone was simply inscribed with, "Rest in Peace." It was written in a different font to Moïse's inscription, and her name was misspelled.

Today, muted orange moss grows at the junction between the upright stone and the massive base stone that bears the name LaGrandeur inscribed in a large uppercase font. The graves lie at the base of a large cottonwood tree with deeply creviced grey bark. Its long branches seem to tenderly embrace the graves below, sheltering them from the glaring sun, the driving rain and snow, and the strong west wind.

THE STORY BEHIND THE STORY

Some moments in one's life are remarkable and stand out vividly upon reflection. Sometimes these happen by pure chance, sometimes we are drawn to them not knowing the profound effect that they will have on our lives, and maybe sometimes we are in the hands of fate.

After graduation from university, I accepted a job at Canadian Pacific Railway, working as a Reliability Engineer in the Mechanical Department, developing predictive rules for removing cars from service due to issues with bearings, wheels, and air brakes.

Around that time, I became very interested in genealogy and began actively researching my maternal grandfather's family, in particular Julia, my great-great grandmother. Simultaneously, a cousin from the US, whom I'd never met, was also conducting a search into Julia's fate. Pursuing a lead indicating that Julia lived in Pincher Creek, he searched for the name LaGrandeur in that area. He placed a call to my uncle, who passed this information on to my mother, who passed the details on to me.

I immediately contacted this cousin, and after many emails, phone calls, and a few meetings, we began to piece together the puzzle of our family's history.

Although this story is fictional, it is based on my great-great grandmother's life. Julia was born on a farm near the

Iowa-Missouri border into a family of four boys. Her father was a French Canadian who built the first bridge across the Nishnabotna River, near French Village. Her mother, listed as a half-breed on census records of that time, was the granddaughter of the Oglala Sioux Chief, Crow Feather.

Julia's childhood was tragic. When she was just a small child, during a heated exchange at the family's farm, her father killed a man who had repeatedly stolen wheat. Although he was never charged with the murder, Julia's father moved the family across the Missouri River onto the Nemaha Reservation in Nebraska, joining Chief Red Cloud, a relative. However, Red Cloud soon made the decision to send all of the mixed bloods out of the area until the problems with the US military had subsided.

The family, which now included a second daughter and another son, moved north to the Cheyenne River Reservation to live with Julia's grandmother, Her Many Pipes. For some unknown reason, the four older boys were left behind with relatives on the Nemaha Reservation.

When Julia was about eight years old, the family headed west towards Oregon in a covered wagon. On this journey, they met up with Blackfoot, the mortal enemies of the Sioux. Julia's parents were killed, and the children were captured and adopted by the Blackfoot to be raised as their own. The children remained with the Blackfoot until missionaries found them when Julia was a young teenager and took them to Walla Walla, Washington. At some point, Julia met Moïse, and they married in 1872, settling on a farm in Union County, Oregon, before traveling to the North-West Territory in 1881.

Julia and Moïse moved onto their homestead at the confluence of the Old Man River and the Pincher Creek, located below the Brocket Piikani Reservation, in 1884. Before the construction of the railway, the stagecoach travelled the thirty-five miles between

Fort Macleod and Pincher Creek thrice weekly, carrying mail and passengers along the old Macleod Road. This route crossed the Oldman River at the LaGrandeur homestead, which became known as the LaGrandeur Crossing. Julia and Moïse soon established a stopping place at their homestead, where stagecoach horses were changed out, and weary travelers took shelter and enjoyed a tasty meal, amusing stories, and impromptu dances.

However, all this changed with the completion of Canadian Pacific Railway's rail line between Fort Macleod and Pincher Creek. The railway eliminated the need for the stagecoach to carry mail and passengers, and ultimately for a stopping place at LaGrandeur Crossing.

Remarkably, my newfound cousin is a descendant of Julia's oldest brother, one of the boys left behind on the Nemaha Reservation by the parents. The four older boys never knew what became of their parents or younger siblings once they headed west. Equally tragic, Julia's descendants never knew about their Oglala Sioux heritage, as the family chose to bury this information, presumably because of societal prejudices at the time. This meeting with my newfound cousin was indeed remarkable. Without it, many pieces of the puzzle may never have been rediscovered so that the story could be reassembled.

In the spring of 2010, while I was still at Canadian Pacific Railway, I took a job as a Project Engineer within the Medicine Hat Division, an area of land stretching from Calgary south to the US border and from the BC border at the Crowsnest to Swift Current. I was responsible for the maintenance of the track and structures within this area.

Almost as soon as I started work, there was severe flooding from Medicine Hat eastward into Saskatchewan. Water from the Cypress Hills caused significant destruction along Canadian Pacific Railway's mainline. Consequently, my first winter in this position was spent securing the services of contractors and materials to repair many locations along the right-of-way. These included the replacement of a bridge at Maple Creek, Saskatchewan, the repair of scour holes at numerous timber trestle bridges, and general clean up along the right-of-way.

In the spring of 2011, just as the construction season was beginning, more flooding occurred. However, this time it was located farther west, within southern Alberta. Significant damage occurred on the Crowsnest Subdivision, at the Brocket Bridge that spanned the Pincher Creek.

I submitted a request to Canadian Pacific Railway's Corporate Properties group in order to obtain a land title for the Brocket Bridge. As with most locations along Canadian Pacific Railway's right-of-way, access is through an adjacent landowner's property, so my first task was to determine the names and contact information of the adjacent landowners, in order to ask for permission.

In the meantime, I travelled to examine the damage to the bridge. I met my boss and the road master at the crossing east of the bridge, and we hi-railed the remaining distance to the bridge. A hi-rail vehicle has rubber tires and steel wheels, allowing it to move along a road or on the rail track. When we arrived, we got out to take a look. I fought against the west wind as I opened the truck door, then tightened the inner band on my bright orange hardhat in order to prevent it from blowing off my head.

Although my family is from southern Alberta, I'd never seen a view quite like this. The vividness of the colours made a deep impression on me. With the recent rain, the green grass was interspersed with yellow buffalo beans, pink wild geraniums, purple shooting stars, and the small, fragrant, yellow-flowered silver berry. And the view of the mountains in the distance was breathtaking.

I made my way down the steep embankment, along a well-worn cow path, from the track level to the edge of the creek. The steep cut bank protected us from the strong wind. The muddy brown water was still moving swiftly, continually working to cut a new path on the east side of the west pier, eroding the embankment. My boss found a large stick and shimmied his way onto the east side of the west pier. He poked the stick into the water along the edge of the pier and out as far as he could reach in order to estimate the size of the scour hole that had developed. It turned out that the hole was substantial.

When I checked my email inbox later that day, there was a message regarding the land title. I opened it and caught my breath. The adjacent landowners were listed as Moïse and Julia LaGrandeur! This was obviously the original land title.

To this day, I still remember the feeling in my stomach when I read their names. It took some time for the reality to sink in. The Brocket Bridge had been constructed on the homestead of my great-great grandparents! They'd sold part of their homestead to Canadian Pacific Railway and watched the construction of the bridge that I was now tasked with repairing.

I eventually determined the name of the current adjacent landowners and contacted them. After some negotiation, I gained permission to access the bridge through their property and met the landowner on site. After some discussion, the older gentleman mentioned that he was familiar with LaGrandeur Crossing and showed me where the original homestead used to sit. A few decades earlier, Heritage Park in Calgary had expressed interest in moving the house to their historical village site in order to preserve this piece of Alberta's history. However, the house unfortunately caught fire before it could be moved.

During the bridge repair, I spent time on site. As a result of this twist of fate, my life became interconnected with Julia. I was on her land. I was standing in her creek. I was breathing her air. The grass and the wildflowers were there in Julia's time. And looking upstream from the bridge at the steep banks of the creek, I saw the old evergreens and the birds soaring overhead. I remember staring up at the bridge from creek-level, at the massive concrete pier rising out of the water and at the beautiful steel members intricately riveted together. I remember watching trains pass over the bridge and hearing the sound echoing through the valley below. It was haunting. And I wondered if this was how Julia felt?

As a small child, I remember visiting a farm west of Fort Macleod with my mother and grandfather, Edouard's son. We were there to place two small white crosses on a hill, to mark the graves of two small children buried there. Sadly, I only found out just recently, following an exhaustive search through old church records and newspapers, that these children were Alexandre and Victorine, and that they passed away from diphtheria.

The Brocket Bridge symbolizes many things to me. I was provided with the opportunity to preserve a one hundred-year-old structure, a bridge linking Julia's world with mine and Julia's future with my past. This beautiful structure likely signified great change in Julia's world. In my world, it signifies my roots and keeps Julia's memory alive. It reminds me to keep moving forward. Despite all of the tragedy that Julia experienced in her life, she never gave up. The bridge symbolizes hope.

This story is loosely based on Julia's life. I've tried to keep the story accurate in terms of locations and dates and the actual events in Julia's life. However, since she passed away many years before I was born, and since this story was written over thirty years after my grandfather's death, the story is fictional. It is my account of what Julia's life may have been like.

ABOUT THE AUTHOR

As a descendant of an early pioneering family, in what would become the province of Alberta, Lara Malmqvist grew up hearing the colourful tales of the early southern Alberta settlers, living in an untamed landscape richly steeped in history and rapidly changing with the westward expansion of the railroad. That early family would become the inspiration for *Twelve Horses for Julia*.

An engineer by trade, Lara lives in the windswept, rolling foot-hills of Southern Alberta—where the brave pioneers she writes about carved out lives for their families so long ago—with her two kids, three horses, and six cats (at last count).

Twelve Horses for Julia is her first book of historical fiction.

Lightning Source UK Ltd.
Milton Keynes UK
UKHW011444170220
358851UK00005B/1670